D0104799

ALSO BY THE AUTHOR

Once the Shore

SNOW HUNTERS

A NOVEL

PAUL YOON

SIMON & SCHUSTER
New York London Toronto Sydney New Delhi

Simon & Schuster
1230 Avenue of the Americas
New York, NY 10020

First Simon & Schuster hardcover edition August 2013

Designed by Joy O'Meara

Manufactured in the United States of America

10 9 8 7 6 5 4 3 2 1

Library of Congress Cataloging-in-Publication Data

Yoon, Paul.
Snow hunters : a novel / Paul Yoon. — First Simon & Schuster hardcover edition.
pp. cm.
1. Korean War, 1950–1953—Veterans—Fiction. 2. Refugees—Korea (North)—Fiction. 3. Brazil—Emigration and immigration—Korea (North) 4. Loneliness—Fiction. I. Title.
PS3625.O54S66 2013
813'.6—dc23 2012048365

ISBN 978-1-4767-1481-3
ISBN 978-1-4767-1483-7 (ebook)

for Laura, my coast

I saw a tree inside a tree
rise kaleidoscopically

as if the leaves had livelier ghosts.

—CHRISTIAN WIMAN

Children in the trees,

one falling
into the grip of another

—MICHAEL ONDAATJE

I

1

That winter, during a rainfall, he arrived in Brazil.

He came by sea. On the cargo ship he was their only passenger. In the last days of the ship's journey it had grown warm and when he remarked that there was no snow, the crew members laughed. They had been throwing fish overboard, as they always did, for luck, and he watched as the birds twisted their bodies in the wind and dove. He had never seen the ocean before, had never journeyed so far as he had in this month alone. He was called Yohan and he was twenty-five years old.

He was dressed in an old gray suit that was too large for him and wore a hat with a short brim. They were not his clothes. They had been given to him at the camp and after he had changed, the young nurse, an American, took the military shirt he had worn for all those years and folded it with care even though it was torn and stale, no longer recognizable.

The nurse had thin shoulders, he remembered, and her neck had darkened from the sun. She had been kind to him. Through all the days at the camp there had been that. But he did not tell her so and he said his farewells to the guards and the doctors who stood in a line under the tent in that long field where the sky was always low and vast and where there was always a wind that carried the smell of the soil and sickness and the sound of animals from a nearby farm.

He was escorted into the back of a UN truck. It had snowed the night before but the day was clear as he left. From a tower someone waved. He shut his eyes and thought of castles.

He had also been given a rucksack with a spare shirt and trousers. A letter confirming his residence and his employment was in his jacket pocket, tucked behind a folded handkerchief.

It was close to dawn, and the ship was near land, when the rain began to fall. The rain was slow and light and they all remained on deck. Yohan felt the drops tap the brim of his hat and vanish along his shoulders. His eyes were dry and red from the wind. The night before, facing a mirror in a cabin, he had clipped his hair short, the way the nurses had often cut his hair in the camp, checking for lice. He had also shaved, unsure at first whether he remembered how, hesitating before pressing the razor against his skin.

He could see now the coast. It resembled a cloud at first. Then it changed and the line broke into segments and he saw the tiles of rooftops and the stone and the whitewashed walls following the slope of a tall hill.

The port grew visible. Then the sails and the masts of ships. He gripped the railing and followed the smoke from the steamers rising above the town.

Near the peak he could make out a church spire and higher, on the open ridge, a single large tree. Farther up the coast, to the north, a plantation house stood in a long field. And farther still, on a headland, a lighthouse was flashing.

They entered the harbor. As the ship approached a pier they were surrounded by a low fog and the sudden echo of voices and engines and the strains of ropes against pulleys. Merchants were looking up at them, motioning their arms and lifting the goods that they were selling. Fishermen were cleaning their boats; landowners were preparing to journey farther west, to visit their farms and their tenants.

He said the name of this country and then said it again.

The ship docked and he helped the men unload their shipment. He kept his eyes focused on the ship, on the crates sliding down the gangplank. He felt movement behind him, heard a slow hammering. He caught the scent of blood but was unsure whether it was his imagination or from all the fishing nets moving through the air.

The rain had not stopped and one of the sailors, the oldest of them, offered him an umbrella. It was blue with a wooden handle.

The sailor shrugged and grinned and said, —From the child, and pointed up at the ship where Yohan thought he saw a crown of hair and the length of a pale scarf gliding along the sky. A young boy was running after her, waving, and from that distance Yohan caught the voice of the girl, its delicacy and assuredness, the way it rose like a kite, the foreign cadence of words in another language.

He paused, as though expecting something. But then they were gone and he was unsure whether he had seen or heard them at all, unsure whether he had understood the sailor correctly. There were no other passengers, he was told.

—To a good life, the sailor said now, and Yohan shook hands with them all, catching the fatigue in their oil-stained faces, these men whom he had lived with for over a month and who had made an effort to keep him company on that ship, teaching him card games, sharing their cigarettes, telling him what little they knew of the country where they had just arrived.

The sailors were South Korean. In the war they had been in the navy and there had been times during the trip when they gathered on the deck in the evenings as the weather grew warm and they passed around a bottle and told him of the fighting at sea. But then they looked at one another and then at Yohan and grew silent.

They spoke instead of their lives now and the families they started, how they had been shipping cargo for a year and how they had moved to Japan, where there was more work to be found.

—And wives, one of the sailors had said, approaching the edge of the deck.

In his hand he held the bottle they had been drinking from, a long wick slipped into it, then the spark of a match. His hand aglow as he threw the bottle into the night, the momentary flare in the sky, then that brief explosion and Yohan hiding his body's reaction to the noise and the sailors shouting up at that vast dark they traveled through.

Now, on the pier, a month later, he did not want to part with them. He lingered close, listening to them speak in Korean, not knowing when he would hear it again. But there was nothing more to say and so he looked at them one last time and waved.

He left the harbor and made his way inland, sheltered by his new umbrella, following a narrow road into a neighborhood of apartments and shops. Alone now, he stared at all the street markers and the hanging signs, his body suddenly overwhelmed by the noises of a town, its new smells, an unknown language.

The sailors had taught him as much Portuguese as they could, what little they themselves had learned, but he could no longer remember the words and the phrases, his mind searching for some remnant but unable to find one, unable to focus and settle as he followed the road.

The town was large, almost a city, and opened out along the rise of the hill. As he moved farther into the town he felt its density, its height. He kept looking up at the unfamiliar architecture, the designs of gates and entrances, the high floors. Buildings were the color of seashells. The dark windows everywhere like a thousand doors in the land.

A girl on a bicycle approached and he stepped onto the sidewalk as she sped past him, throwing newspapers against closed entrances. He paused, caught by a memory. He had not seen a bicycle in years. The rain lifted off the wheels as the girl pedaled farther away. A light appeared inside a bakery, then the smoke from a thin flue on the roof.

He stopped a fisherman, showing him a business card, and the man pointed toward the ridge and motioned his arm to the right. He followed a cobblestone road, turning at a barbershop and continuing along another road that moved around the slope, past row houses with narrow, brightly painted shutters. He began to notice paper signs on the windows, written in Japanese.

The tailor's shop stood between an apartment and a pharmacy. The building was whitewashed and two stories tall. There was no sign. There were instead two large windows through which he could see tables, rolls of fabric, and a tailor's dummy with a measuring tape draped around the shoulders of its headless body.

It was early in the morning. From across the street he looked up at the second-floor windows.

And it was there, standing in front of the tailor's shop, as the rain fell, that he felt the tiredness of his journey for the first time. He heard the rush of a storm drain and his legs weakened and he grew dizzy. He gripped the umbrella and thought of the years that had passed and were an ocean away now. He thought of Korea and the war there and he thought of the camp near the southern coast of that country, beside an airbase, where he had been a prisoner for two years. He thought of the day he woke and saw the trees and then the men with their helmets and their weapons swaying around him like chimes.

The Americans called them northerners and those first weeks they kept his wrists bound. But then the doctors, in need of men, untied him and the others, and he dug graves and washed clothes in buckets. He carried trays for the nurses and took walks in the yard with Peng or the missionaries who visited, following the high fences, the men in the towers looking down at them.

He slept in a cabin with the other prisoners and in the winters the heat of their bodies kept them warm. Moonlight kept them company, the way it leaked through the timber walls and shifted across them as the hours passed; and sleepless, he thought of his father and all that snow in the winters in that mountain town where Yohan was born and where he had lived and it all seemed so far to him then, as though the earth had expanded, his memories, too, and he could no longer grasp them. And only then, when those thoughts began to recede, fading into a thin line, would he sleep.

He did not know when exactly the war ended. He did not hear of it until some days later.

One day he was told they would return him to his home. To his country, they said. To the north.

—Repatriation, they called it.

He declined their offer. From the camp he was the only one.

So he stayed a while longer, helping the doctors with the ones who were too sick to travel and would not last long. He held the young men's hands if they wanted him to or sat beside them and described the fields and the trees and the clouds, and the young men smiled and thought of their mothers, unable to open their eyes or move their heads. And some wept and said that they were sorry, so very sorry, and he wondered what they were sorry for, but it was all right because in their eyes he could see that they were not looking at him but someone else in the last of their dreams.

And then some time later a man visited.

—From the United Nations, he said, and they gathered around a table under a tent with the nurses and the missionaries.

There was an agreement with Brazil, the man said, and Yohan remained silent. He had never heard that word before. If he wanted to, the man said, for the camp would soon be gone.

—The sun, the nurse beside him said, looking far away where the snow from the trees had begun to scatter. I bet there's so much sun.

And he thought of a place where there would be no more nights.

—Brazil, Yohan said, and the man nodded and the nurse smiled and so he did, too.

There was a tailor there. A Japanese man. Kiyoshi was his name. Yohan would be the tailor's apprentice because he had mended clothes at the camp. He was good at it, the nurse said, and Yohan looked down at his hands, forgetting that when the UN man appeared he had been stooped over the table, under the tent, mending the clothes that had been taken, during that war, from the dead.

It was now 1954. He stood on the sidewalk, holding the blue umbrella.

The rain continued to fall. It fell on the rooftops on the slopes of the hill and in the narrow streets and the alleyways and on the windows of the tailor's shop, blurring the image of his body. The morning was gray and the color of rust. All the sounds of the waking city seemed to rise toward the sky, dissipating as the rain fell.

A puddle began to form on the sidewalk where he stood; the toes of his shoes had grown wet and dark.

He regained his strength. He adjusted his hat and then his rucksack. From his jacket pocket he took out the letter. He crossed the street and knocked once on the glass door. Waiting there, opposite his reflection, his hands shook and he stilled them.

From where he stood outside he could now see the shop in its entirety: a single long room with a dark wood floor, worn pale by footsteps and the legs of chairs and tables; fabrics piled on shelves and leaning against walls stained by cigarette smoke; sewing machines on worktables;

wooden boxes filled with scissors and sewing needles and spools of thread. A portable radio. An old fan with a single lightbulb hanging from the low ceiling.

He leaned closer to the glass. In the back there was a heavy red curtain covering a doorway, framed by a dim light.

It was from there that a man appeared, pushing the curtain to the side. He was short and walked with a stoop. He was wearing an undershirt and a vest and his hair was gray and long, tied in the back with a piece of thread. As the man approached, his slippers hit the floor in a slow rhythm, like the soft pattern of rain against the dome of the umbrella Yohan held.

The man lifted his hand.

—It's open, he called, in Japanese, but continued to approach and, with effort, opened the door himself.

Yohan had not spoken Japanese in some time and he struggled to respond, reaching for a language that seemed to float in a far memory.

—Come in, come in, the man said, and Yohan entered, leaving the umbrella outside by one of the shop windows.

There was no longer the sound of rain, or it had faded, and his ears adjusted now to the low hum of the radio and the ceiling fan. He could smell a broth of some kind, and tea, and he remembered then that he had not eaten since the day before, a small meal with the crew, mindful of their sharing. He was suddenly struck with hunger.

But he remained still. They stood facing each other at the front of the shop, silent until the man's eyes focused on Yohan's suit. The man reached for him and pinched the fabric on each shoulder.

—I see the problem, the tailor said.

Yohan took out the letter and bowed. The man slipped on a pair of reading glasses that he kept in his vest pocket.

While he read, Yohan studied the man's face: his calm eyes, his thick lips, the old and dark skin that had spent years under the sun.

This was Kiyoshi, in his expression a patience and also a steadiness Yohan would grow accustomed to over the years.

The tailor folded the letter and slipped it into his vest pocket along with his reading glasses. He lit a cigarette. He took Yohan's hand. Kiyoshi's fingers were warm and rough.

—Welcome, he said, continuing to speak in Japanese.

He reached for the rucksack, attempted to lift it, but

changed his mind and tapped Yohan on the shoulder, motioning for him to follow.

They headed to the back of the room, passing through the curtain, into a kitchen. A teakettle and a pot of soup were on the stove. Beyond the kitchen there was a door ajar, revealing the corner of a small room: a nightstand, the spine of a book, slippers, and an ashtray, the edge of a cot that reminded him of the field hospital in the camp, the gray light of the morning extending onto the floor.

But they did not go there. They turned and climbed a set of narrow stairs that creaked with each step. They went slowly, Kiyoshi leading and holding on to the handrail, his cigarette smoke lifting toward the dim lights in a slow whirl.

There had been no electricity at the camp, though there was at the military base; and in the evenings when it grew dark and the buildings vanished, a line of electric light appeared beyond the fences, these rows of square shapes in the sky glowing every night. And the dying, who lay in their cots under the tents, would stare out across that distance as though waiting for something else to appear while the doctors made their rounds with lanterns. And Yohan in the cabin thinking of nights in the town wearing his father's coat and watching a lit stage, the long shadows of actors.

There were two small rooms on the second floor, connected by a short hallway. One was used for storage. The tailor brought Yohan to the other one, stopping beside the doorway.

The room was above the shop. The ceiling was sloped so that one wall was taller than the other. A single window looked out onto the street. In the far corner there was a mattress on the floor. Closer to the door, along the high wall, there was a bureau, a chair, and a small desk. Again, there was a lightbulb hanging from the ceiling. That was all.

It had not occurred to him until now that he had been silent since entering the shop. But before he could speak Kiyoshi left. He listened to the old man descend the stairs. He walked across the room, settled his rucksack beside the mattress, and opened the window.

From here he could see broken glass glued onto the rooftops descending the slope of the town; the occasional television antenna; birds on clotheslines, the clothes drenched from the rain, their colors dulled. In the far distance there were the ships in port and the winding streets he had followed to get here, the wet cobblestones and the damp awnings of shops and restaurants.

The girl on the bicycle returned. He leaned out the window and watched her approach. Directly across the street was an apartment building. Beside that were two stores: a bakery and a pastry shop. Without pausing the girl dipped her hand into her shoulder bag and threw. He listened to the impact of the newspaper on each door and the rain in the bicycle wheels.

A moment later Kiyoshi stepped outside, reaching for the paper and for the blue umbrella, too. A group of boys ran by, kicking a rubber ball in the rain, and an old woman, with her head covered in a bright shawl, waited under the awning of the pharmacy.

He took off his suit jacket. He left the window and stood under the lightbulb, examining it. He flipped the switch and it began to flicker and he turned it off. He reached up to tighten it into the socket and tried it again. Then he sat on the mattress. It was hard and a corner was torn. His shirt stank of seawater and fish. Or perhaps it was his skin or his hair.

His tiredness returned to him and he settled into the bed. He shut his eyes. Through the open window he could hear the tapping of the rain and voices and a car and then a ship's horn. A single chime of a church bell. A door opening. A song on the radio. The steady punches of a sewing machine. He heard aircraft and the dust spraying from trucks and the wind against the tents but it was faint and calm and he did not mind. He was riding a bicycle. He felt a hand on the small of his back. Someone familiar spoke to him and he said, —I can go a little longer, and he lifted a shovel and sank it into the earth. A group of children whistled and clapped. And then he was running his hands through a girl's hair and she took his wrist and they moved through a corridor where rows of dresses hung from the ceiling. Those dresses turned into the sea.

When he woke it was dark. The lights from the town had entered the room, the furniture casting shadows. In the far corner, beside the door, a man sat on the desk chair, facing him.

Yohan froze, startled. Then his eyes adjusted and he saw that it was his suit jacket. He did not remember placing it there. He rose, smelling the bowl of soup that was still warm on the desk. Beside it lay an ashtray and a pack of cigarettes.

The fluorescent lights of a store began to blink and the room lit bright and then dimmed. He watched his shadow on the wall behind him appear and fade. The room was thick with warmth. A breeze came and he took off his shirt.

He was not yet used to the heat of this country. It was summer here and he wondered if there existed a different season for every corner of this world in this moment and the moments to come. Whether if you traveled fast and far enough you could witness a year passing in a single journey.

Across the street, a woman stood on a second-floor balcony, looking down. She wore a pale dress that revealed her thin arms, and her dark hair hung down across her shoulders. A motorbike paused below her, its engine running. The man was looking up. Together they spoke in a language Yohan did not yet know but would learn and he concentrated on the soft cadence, again trying to remember the words and phrases the sailors had taught him.

And then his eyes scanned the landscape, consuming it.

He would learn the streets and the buildings of this hill town that resembled the old shell of some creature. And he would know the people who moved within it.

He lifted his suit jacket, examining the shoulders and

the sleeves. He tried it on. It was no longer too large for him; the shoulders had been altered, the sleeves, too.

The beam of the lighthouse swept across the harbor. In the sea there were stars. Millions of them, reflected in the water's surface. The rain had stopped.

2

From that day on he woke early. Kiyoshi waited for him in the kitchen, where he boiled water for tea. Then they took their cups and the teapot and passed through the curtain into the shop.

The tailor had moved the worktables toward each wall so that they worked with their backs facing each other. At the camp Yohan had used a machine with a hand crank; in the shop there were treadles and he was at first unaccustomed to the movement of his foot.

Kiyoshi gave him fabric to practice on. He spent those first days adjusting his body to that foreign rhythm, his foot in constant motion as his hands pushed the cloth forward. On occasion Kiyoshi stood behind him, peering over his shoulder, though Yohan did not look up.

On the wall in front of him, on a shelf, there were packages wrapped in tan paper and twine. The tailor reached for one and placed it on his own table until the bell above the door chimed and a customer entered. They talked for a moment, pleasantries, and then Kiyoshi handed the person the package.

Yohan would not know until later that they were unlabeled and he would be impressed by the tailor's memory of who wore what.

In the town they lived on the outskirts of a Japanese community. Most of their customers were their neighbors and the diplomats who visited from Tokyo, ordering their suits every season or bringing in their old ones for them to mend and widen.

Every so often a man appeared from elsewhere in the town, lured by Kiyoshi's prices, a lawyer or landowners or men who worked in the government offices. They talked often, unused to keeping still, and Yohan would remain silent, unable to understand them, catching only a few words as the tailor measured them.

He always stood to the side: measuring tapes draped over his neck and a pencil and a notepad in his shirt pocket. Sometimes children pressed their foreheads against the windows and watched. They made faces and waved and Yohan waved back.

Other days the farmers came, asking Kiyoshi to mend a shirt or a pair of trousers, paying with grains and vegetables. There were also wives who came for dresses, women who, upon meeting Yohan for the first time, said, —Oh my, where did you find him? And they flirted with him and asked if he could measure them, lifting their arms and tilting their waists.

He blushed as Kiyoshi translated for him and laughed, lighting the women's cigarettes. They liked him even more because Yohan did not answer them when they asked about his crooked nose and the thin scar across the bridge.

They were not always in the shop. The tailor took him to the port where twice a season a ship arrived from Japan with fabrics and silks. Some days he found the crew who had brought him here, and it made him happy to see them. The older one asked about the umbrella and grinned. Yohan still had it, still used it, and the sailor laughed because it was a lady's umbrella, he said.

The crew placed the fabrics on a dolly, and they said their good-byes and Yohan pushed the dolly over the cobblestone and up the hill as Kiyoshi walked behind him, pausing at times to view the displays of a shop window.

The tailor delivered clothes as well throughout the town. But as the months passed he did so less often. Yohan took his place, carrying mended shirts and new dresses and suits and even gloves or a hat that needed repair, each wrapped in the tan paper and twine.

There was a bicycle at the shop but Yohan never used it. Instead he walked through the narrow streets and the alleyways. He stopped often, shying away from the passersby, searching for the numbers on the doors and looking up at the street signs, making sure that the words matched the ones on the slip of paper he held.

At first he stayed within the borders of the Japanese community. In doing so, day by day, he grew accustomed to his neighborhood and the people who lived nearby. Then, as the months passed and his energy returned to him, he began to venture farther into the town. He went from neighborhood to neighborhood, gradually, delivering clothes to older customers who had known Kiyoshi since he first came.

He passed structures he had never seen before: a gated mansion, fountains, and sculptures in gardens.

Others were familiar to him: a single-story cottage, the brick wall of someone's property, the market squares.

He stood in front of the entrances to apartment buildings, unsure of whether to knock or press a buzzer. He climbed winding staircases and stopped at each landing to look out the slim windows. He waited in a foyer with his hands in his pockets, hiding his nervousness as the retired Portuguese attaché looked through a drawer to pay him.

Once a month he drank tea with a widow. For half an hour he sat in her living room on her expensive furniture as she spoke to him and he nodded, struggling, pretending to grasp what she said.

In these homes he looked discreetly around at the rooms, glancing at the cleanliness of the windows, his eyes falling upon a painting or a pet: a cat on a bookshelf, birds in cages, a pair of dogs lying under a table, lifting their ears on occasion to listen to the maid in the kitchen. If there was pottery on a shelf or a cabinet, a vase or a bowl, he lingered over it, studying the design before leaving.

He delivered clothes to the church as well. It was the highest building in that hill town, closest to the ridge, standing where the road ended and the fields began. He remained by the gate until the groundskeeper appeared from the back, where he lived in a cottage not far from the cemetery.

He was called Peixe by the town because his family had been fishermen, though none were alive anymore. He had been the only one who never fished, never entered the water.

When he was a child he had suffered from polio. His mother, who had once been a customer of Kiyoshi's, used to volunteer at the church and so he spent many of his days there, keeping her company, hiding under the pews.

He walked with a cane and there was a slow grace to his movements. He laughed easily. He was thirty-two years old and had been here all his life. His hair was dark and, like the tailor, he kept a pair of reading glasses in his shirt pocket.

They shook hands and Peixe invited him inside, as he always did, and Yohan smiled, bowing, and returned down the road.

The townspeople no longer expected the tailor but his young apprentice, as they began to call him, with both affection and curiosity. Sometimes he received tips. When he gave them to Kiyoshi, the man shook his head, pushing away Yohan's hand.

He kept the money in a tin box he found in an alleyway one afternoon. On its lid there was an illustration of a woman in an apron carrying a baking tray, a mother, he supposed, with a blue ribbon tied around her hair and words above the image written in English. Every now and then, in his bedroom, he leaned over his desk and lifted the top of the box, smelling the cookies it had once contained.

He found many things in the alleys: a cup, a pocketknife, a shaving brush, a new handkerchief in its box. He stopped often in these narrow streets, a compulsion from childhood when he would search the town for things to barter with the peddlers who visited. He would climb the wheels of their carts and peer down at the treasure, searching for shoelaces, a ball, a knife.

But in those alleyways there were times when he found himself leaning against a wall, not knowing where he was. His hands moved as though he were tearing something. His eyes far away and gone.

It did not last long. It was as though the world he saw cracked, revealing memories he had forgotten. Those small stars. A girl sitting in an empty window frame in a destroyed town they were passing through. How she wiped the dirt off a pear wedge, showing the dark spaces where her teeth had been. A man's hat and a cane lay on the street below her. Peng picked them up, settling the hat on his head and twirling the cane. He gave Yohan his rifle. He then spread mud above his lips, furrowed his eyebrows, waved to her, and wobbled across the street without bending his knees like that funny man they had heard of named Charlie Chaplin.

He thought of those days with Peng, the two of them in their weather-stained uniforms and their helmets and their boots stuffed with newspaper and straw. Peng, that old friend who was three years older and taller than he was, with the odd thin stripe of gray in his hair since he was a child, like the mark of some animal. Even in the war he still moved like some dancer across the hills, ignoring the rain, agile and calm. And Yohan always close behind him, not once losing sight of the shape of Peng's shoulders.

He thought of all the other men and women they had together seen wandering the country, sometimes with the companionship of animals, a slow-moving dog or a mule or once even a gray bird that an old man carried in a handkerchief. It had been injured from a bombing and Yohan remembered the man sitting on the road beside them as they rested, unraveling the handkerchief, delicately, as his mouth chewed on a nut that someone had dropped on the street. Then he placed the chewed mash on his finger and fed the bird that could not fly though its body hummed; and he let Yohan place his hand on its breast and the soft pulse jolted him.

He wondered if the war there had truly ended. He did not know. There was no one to tell him so. There was the news on the radio but Kiyoshi never listened, preferring the stations with music instead, the orchestras.

And he wondered about the wars that had been fought here and he grew embarrassed because he did not know. They did not speak of such things. Nor did they speak of the war that had preceded this one, and he did not know if the tailor had fought in it. It was as though Kiyoshi and the shop had always been here.

Though they were together often, he shared little with Yohan. And he himself did not tell the tailor about his own years. And yet he found comfort in this absence of telling.

He learned about the tailor by what the old man pointed to, what his eyes fell on; by what he ate and how; by his knowledge of fabrics and by the way he avoided certain pedestrians and grinned at others.

From their reticence grew a kind of intimacy. Kiyoshi, who could be seen through the shop window all day with his stooped shoulders, hemming a pair of trousers or replacing the buttons of a shirt. And Yohan across from him, working as well.

Once, Kiyoshi, without turning, asked him what he had found that day and Yohan, surprised, paused. From his jacket pocket he took out a cup someone had thrown away in an alley and Kiyoshi stood to examine it under the light.

—Ah, he said. Good, and then returned it to him.

He said nothing else. They continued to sew and stitch.

Later, they closed the shop together. They went through the day's transactions and reminded each other that a shipment from overseas would arrive the next morning. They ate by their sewing machines, drinking tea and listening to the orchestra on the radio, and soon the tailor fell asleep on his chair.

As the old man slept Yohan continued to organize the fabrics on the shelves, looping thread over a spool and returning scissors and sewing needles to their boxes. He lowered the volume on the radio.

He approached the tailor's dummy, bent forward, studied the shape of its chest, the flatness of its severed arms and head. Wondering if it had been modeled on an actual person. The lights of the streetlamps and the store signs brightened the closed shutters.

His days passed in this way. He learned how to navigate the town. He began to learn the language, listening to the people on the streets and in the shop and to the commercials on the radio.

Sometimes, as they worked, Kiyoshi surprised him by saying aloud a Portuguese word. Yohan repeated it. *Alteração. Medir. Roupa.*

Then, in the late evenings, alone in his room upstairs, Yohan lay on the mattress and spoke, turning a word or a phrase in his mouth as though it were a stone. *Dois. Sopa. Noite. A loja está fechada. A loja está fechada. Noite. Dois. Janela.*

He placed his hands under his head and looked up at the water-stained ceiling, listening to his own voice, which sounded unfamiliar to him, and searching for the rhythm of that new language. He fell asleep with the tip of his tongue against the back of his front teeth.

On other nights, after closing the shop, he and Kiyoshi went up to the roof, bringing chairs, and shared a bottle of wine. They looked out over the hill town and at the movement on the streets and through the windows of apartment buildings: a man on a rocking chair; a child staring back at them; a couple dancing in their bedroom under the relief of a ceiling fan.

There were often power outages in the town and on those nights they stayed on that roof in the dark, in the company of a distant trumpet or a guitar or the ticking of playing cards wedged into bicycle wheels.

They waited for their eyes to adjust, the candles to appear in the windows, then they spent that last hour of the day playing a game, the tailor placing a hand by his ear or pointing; and in Portuguese, Yohan would attempt to identify what they were listening to, or watching.

Once, they heard someone singing on the street. It was a birthday song. They waited for the song to end and then Kiyoshi, drinking his wine, asked when his birthday was. Yohan confessed that he could not remember.

The following week he woke to find a garment bag hanging on his door. He opened it. It was a new suit, made of light cotton, the color of sand. On a notecard, in Japanese, it said: *For another year*.

The suit fit him perfectly. He did not realize until later that afternoon that it was the day he had come to the shop for the first time.

And so he began to think of that day as when one

year turned into another. Kiyoshi seemed to as well. Each year he made Yohan an article of clothing, leaving it in his bedroom, a new pair of trousers or a shirt, sometimes both. Years from now, long after Kiyoshi was gone, he would be wearing the same clothes. He would sit beside his worktable in the evenings and mend the tears in the collars and the shirt cuffs himself. When exactly the old man made them he never discovered.

3

There were hundreds of them.

In the summers they wore what was left of their uniforms. In the winters they were given gray sweaters and coats.

They had chores and duties. They were sent to the field tents to carry the bodies of men who had been captured and who had not survived. That hour surrounded by the sound of scissors and liquid in cups and bowls and jars. The activity of flies. Men with untreated bullet wounds attempted to stay standing as they waited in a line. Men lay in the backs of trucks, their mouths pooling with the afternoon rain.

They were sent to an old textile mill at the edge of the camp where there was another ward. They were told to move the dead as quickly as possible because they needed the beds. If their clothes were salvageable, they were told to take those, too, along with the blankets, and they boiled them in large pots outside with the handle of a broken broom. They scrubbed the blood off mattresses. The clothes they hung on ropes that had been tied across the trees.

They picked root vegetables from a garden the Americans were attempting to cultivate. They carried the potatoes and the carrots and the radishes and the turnips to the cooks.

They worked all day, in silence, stopping only a few times to rest. They worked into the night. From across that distance Yohan could see a pair of silhouettes thrown against the curtain by a light, their bodies the size of the forest trees, their crooked limbs moving over the shape on the cot that bent and shook and went still.

That first week he vomited daily.

And every day, from the clearing, he watched as Peng walked a footpath with his hands raised, his eyes covered in dressings, learning the geography of the prison camp while a guard escorted him.

This young man who had been a part of his childhood and whom he had met again during wartime.

One winter evening, in a railroad car heading south, his face had been like all the faces, worn and unrecognizable. His eyes like all their eyes. Their shoulders bumped. And then he took his helmet off and the moonlight caught the gray stripe in his hair.

Yohan had nearly reached for it, as though it were the warmth of a fire, unraveled by the memory of a boy who used to appear in his town in a caravan, performing magic tricks in the market square, the elderly placing their palms on the boy's head for luck.

As children, they had seen each other only a few times a year at most, and they had not thought of each other until that moment. And yet, on that night, on that train, they had embraced fiercely, unwilling to let go, laughing, waking the other men and almost losing their rifles, their legs swaying out the car into the air.

This momentary bridge. The wonder of a shared memory, returned. Of a place once theirs and a life that had already been lived.

A year later, that gray now gone and their heads shaved. And a town and its market square even farther away than it was. Each day, Peng, with bandages wrapped over his eyes, took Yohan's elbow and worked beside him, asking him about the distances from one building to another, from the graves to the garden, his mind growing accustomed to that new dark.

The days were unchanging. They witnessed the arrival of more prisoners and more men carrying stretchers through the gates, their legs hidden in the tall grass and the wounded floating on their backs across the field. The guards rotating in the towers. The occasional storm of a helicopter and all the dust, and all of them looking up from where they had been working, watching the thing rise.

They stood in line for the food that was given to them in tin bowls and Yohan used his fingers to eat and tasted the salt and the dirt of his skin.

There were times when he fed Peng, who, in his exhaustion, was unable to leave the prisoner cabin, growing confused in his blindness as to where he was. Sometimes, in his half-sleep, he asked of his family or the farm Yohan had once lived on, or whether it was time to put on a show.

He watched Peng's lips move and felt the tiredness of the day in his shoulders and his feet and from the barracks a fire was lit and some nights he heard singing as the light in the mountains faded.

They slept beside each other. He woke every hour to the sound of Peng scratching the bandages over his eyes and gently took his wrist until he stopped. Some nights the men in the cabin would also be awake and he listened to them speak of their homes, of food, the turning of their stomachs from hunger. Or the incomprehensible words of someone dreaming, a puzzle made of a phrase, of sounds, and the man within a maze.

He listened to other men cry and he knew that they were covering their mouths and he did nothing. He lay against the wall, his foot brushing someone's head. He stared up at a hole in the ceiling where in the winters the snow would fall, once building a mound on someone's stomach the size of a child's palm.

He wondered what choice there was in what was remembered; and what was forgotten.

There were moments when it seemed possible that they would survive, that all of them would.

But there were also times when the hours slipped away and he no longer knew how many days had passed. When his mouth grew numb and he lost his sense of taste. When he could not stop shivering in the cold and Peng held him, his body cocooned in a blanket. He listened to the footsteps of the guards and watched the shadows they cast into the cabin, circling the floor and the walls, this slow carousel that would not end. He pressed his forehead against the wall, straining to see a corner of a field, the web of a fence. He longed to listen to a song. To breathe deeply. He grabbed Peng, pushing his hands through what little there was of his hair, as though in search of something. He shouted, waking everyone, until he lost his voice. He ran in place, lifting his legs as high as he could, or turned in circles until he grew dizzy, a delirious energy in his fingers, Peng reaching into the dark and trying to calm him until the guards took him outside and beat him. He lay in the clearing, unable to rise, his body illuminated by the electric lights of the perimeter. He opened his eyes, in that brief moment, with two weapons pointed at him, and felt the unexpected joy of glimpsing the stars.

In the winters the wounded were sent to the textile mill. Broken windows were covered with wood and blankets. There had been tables and looms in the workspaces, long abandoned. Portable sewing machines were discovered in a closet.

Now there was a sea of beds. Birds nesting in the high rafters. A cup of medicine was passed from convalescent to convalescent to reach a boy in the far corner, who lay still and turned his head to watch the slow procession of arms in the air. In the sunlight, against the frosted window glass, there was a wall of indecipherable drawings made by a sleepless hand.

They stood in a line, waiting for a doctor to check their health, their teeth, their eyes. They had been shoveling snow all day. A skin infection had begun near Peng's wounds. Yohan watched a doctor feed him a pill and unravel the bandages.

While he was cleaning Peng's face, a bird descended. It flew low over the beds, collecting stray hairs, and he heard laughter. He saw Peng tilt his head, grow alert. It circled, turned, and Peng remained motionless as it flew past him, this sudden movement beside his ear.

That winter Peng's energy had begun to slow. He grew hesitant in his movements, and disoriented, forgetting where a building was. There were times when it took him a moment to respond.

He used to share with Yohan all the places he had seen, all his performances, keeping them distracted from the cold and their hunger. But the moments when they were reminded of their years as children had grown farther apart.

When he tried to clean Peng's wounds, as the doctor told him to, rubbing a wet cloth over his face, Peng flicked his arm away.

Once, Yohan turned to find him gone, only to see him later crouched behind the cabins. He had unwrapped his bandages and was rocking on his heels, digging his fingernails into his head, a thin stream of blood following the line of his jaw.

—It itches, he said, his breath visible in the air, and Yohan reached for him, waiting for his body to calm.

One night they woke to find their shoulders pinned against the floor. Prisoners surrounded them. With the weight of three men on him, he watched Peng struggle as a pair of hands pushed down against his forehead. They ripped off his bandages. They inspected his dead eyes. They pressed their faces as close as they could to his and moved their fingers in front of him. Unable to understand what was happening, Peng's head twitched. The fear centered on his lips.

They stripped him of his clothes. They found some food he had been hiding. They took everything.

There had been a wager to see if Peng was really blind.

He spent the morning in his coat and nothing else

until a guard, his amusement fading, found him a spare set of clothes. There were no spare boots and so they took turns wearing Yohan's. He was given dressings to wrap over his feet. The rest he wrapped over his eyes.

Crossing a field that afternoon, Peng stopped. He looked out toward the mill.

He said, —I'm waiting for someone to die. For a dead man's boots.

Then he dropped the bucket of water he had been carrying and pressed his hands against his face and his shoulders shook. In the field the water spread and froze. And Yohan, for a moment, was unable to move, looking down, shocked at the sudden appearance of their reflection.

A doctor once wrote Yohan's name on a piece of paper, in English, with a pencil, and gave it to him, though whether that was how it was spelled the doctor did not know, he had guessed. Yohan slipped the paper into his shirt pocket and in the nights he would open it and stare at his name written in another language for the first time. And he would memorize the letters, saying each one in silence, extending the muscles of his tongue, his mouth even then forming shapes unfamiliar to him.

It was how he would spell his name; he would use those letters the doctor had imagined for him and call them his own.

All these faces he no longer remembered, just some of the parts. Where they had been and how they were wounded, whom he buried and who lived, all of them the years could not retain. They were now remnants. How he once watched a man bring a ladle of water to a friend's cracked lips. How a man, naked in the winter, washed himself in a corner with the warmth of the used laundry water. Two men once attempted to escape, only to return the next day with their wrists bound. How one of them reached for the guard's rifle and placed it into his mouth.

How clean were the eyes of the dead.

In that last year, long after Peng was gone, he was brought to a table where there was a basket of clothes and a sewing machine. And that doctor who had written his name showed him how to operate the machine and then headed toward the corner of the field tent to rest, sitting on a wooden chair with a book on his lap. In the warmer nights he slept there because it was easier, because there were not enough of them for the shifts.

And as Yohan mended whatever clothes he could, trying and starting over, the doctor read aloud from the book so that the guards and the wounded could hear as well, and they all turned to him as he flipped the pages with his stained fingers.

In those times, in that vast tent in the field, there was only his voice, a steady wind, the whistle of glass, and a story.

II

4

In the fall, Yohan climbed to the top of the hill town. He passed the church where the road ended and crossed a sloped meadow, heading toward the tree on the ridge.

The tree was tall and had been shaped by the wind. Its branches were long and thick, extending out in one direction. Some nearly touched the ground.

He rested there, on the peak of the hill, and looked out at the distant lighthouse and the old plantation house to the north. Breakers approached a cliff. The wind was steady, consuming the noises, and he watched the town go about its day.

It was his second year here. He had grown accustomed to the heat and the warmer seasons. His skin had darkened and his muscles had returned to him. He kept his hair short, walking with Kiyoshi to the barbershop every few weeks.

Earlier that day he had gone to the market in the large square overlooking the port. He walked through the aisles, passing the stalls, listening to the vendors and the shoppers converse and barter, translating what sentences he could in his mind, catching a phrase he did not yet understand and memorizing the sounds so that he could ask Kiyoshi about it later.

Craftsmen and toy makers sat on wicker chairs, fanning themselves with newspapers. They sold pottery and dolls and tapestries and wooden animals and toy boats of various sizes, lined up in rows, some of them as small as a pebble. He held the miniature rowboats, examined their craft, felt their lightness and their smoothness in his palm. He bent down and peered into their hollows as though expecting to find something there. He imagined each of them being placed into the sea, moving in separate directions. He thought how wonderful it would be to follow them.

The full height of the church spire rose above the ridge. He heard a door open and looked down into the town, over a stone wall where the old priest appeared, followed by Peixe, who leaned on his cane as they walked through the garden behind the church. He understood that they were speaking about a Sunday service and a dinner, catching their fragmented conversation. Then they parted, the priest returning inside as the groundskeeper began to collect vegetables.

Peixe wore cotton trousers, an old shirt, and a vest. His hair was disheveled and there was a basket slung over his arm. In that first year in the town, they had only spoken a few words.

There had been a farmer who sometimes visited the camp, bartering with the soldiers. He lived in a farmhouse in the valley, far beyond the fences, and Yohan would look out at it from time to time, seeing the farmer at the door or outside, washing a window.

He never knew the man, did not know if he was married or had a family, or how his life had been altered during that war. He imagined the man was still there. Perhaps even the camp itself. He thought of all the doctors and soldiers and nurses forever moving along that field surrounded by high fences and towers, and he wondered what remained in those mountains.

From the ridge he watched Peixe for a while, in the afternoon stillness, the garden trees throwing shadows on him.

In the harbor, crates hung suspended in the air. Birds circled them. The sea was clear. It moved toward him and faded and he felt the time that had passed and his time here. He thought that he had made the best of it all, that he had worked and made a living, and he felt the contentment of that. He thought of what the years would bring, what sort of life was left in him.

It was then that he saw the children. There were two of them, a boy and a girl. They had appeared on the cliff beside the town. Now they were moving through the meadow, heading toward him.

Their clothes were almost identical. They both wore trousers that were too large for them, the hems rolled up to their shins and wet from the ocean. They wore white button-down shirts: the girl had folded her sleeves up to her elbows; the boy's hung over his arms so that it appeared as though he were without hands, the pale fabric swinging by his hips as he followed the girl.

The boy had short, dark hair; the girl's was long and pale and fell down her shoulders, reaching her waist. They were barefoot.

He knew them. Though he had not seen them in some time.

He watched as they slowed in front of him and approached with shyness. He was sitting against the tree with his hands around his knees. They stopped and the boy looked somewhere behind Yohan's shoulder as if expecting someone else to appear. The girl's eyes were fixed on him but revealed nothing. The day was bright and the wind continued to come in from the sea.

He held up a bag. The girl tilted her head, as though considering the bag, then took it. Her arm vanished into the opening, her hand burrowing in the canvas. When it reappeared it held bread rolls, fruit, and strips of dried fish he had gotten at the market.

She handed the bag back to him. Then, standing there under the tree, the boy and the girl began to eat. He watched them bringing their hands to their lips and their mouths work the food and their eyes calm as they began to look around at the slope and the rooftops of the town, enjoying their meal, their shyness now gone, replaced by an ease, some kind of comfort, almost, though whether he was a part of that he did not know.

The girl tucked her hair behind her ears. He could smell them, their clothes, their hair, and their breaths. They smelled of paint and the shore.

When they were finished they wiped their hands on their shirts and moved past him. They reached for a low limb in the tree. The boy raised a calloused foot. The girl hung in the air, swinging. Then they began to climb. Their bodies circled the tree like planets as they went higher, blocking the afternoon light.

In the middle of the tree they each took a branch and rested, dangling their legs above him. The boy faced the sea and the girl the farmlands and the distant mountains. They sat hidden among the branches; patches of their clothes were visible, the girl's long hair, an ankle and a foot. One of them coughed and then they were quiet.

Now there was just the sound of the leaves. The boy lay down against a branch and Yohan, below them, extended his legs and leaned against the tree. He shut his eyes.

He heard the girl say, —Do you still have it?

She spoke in Portuguese, that language he was still learning. He hesitated, repeating her question in his mind.

Then, without looking at her, he nodded.

From the tree he heard laughter. Her quiet delight. He smiled. He used to think that he had dreamed them on that first day, the sailor pointing up toward the deck of a ship and handing him an umbrella.

It stood in the corner of his room, its fabric long dry from the last time it had rained.

He heard her sigh, the boy shift and settle.

Then she said his name. She said it slowly, taking her time with the syllables. She said it once. He kept his eyes closed. Her voice as he remembered it, that kite of sound settling into him. Then nothing more was said and they stayed for a while longer on that hill.

In those years they slipped in and out of his life.

He did not know where the children came from, whether they had been born here or had arrived from somewhere else. He knew only that some days they appeared and that there were also days when he did not see them at all. Sometimes they stayed in the town for a full year. Other times they stayed for a month or a season and no one knew when, or if, they would ever come back. But they always did.

He was unaware of where they went. And he wondered whether there were others in the far towns who knew them and had grown accustomed to them, even expected them, just as he began to.

At one time he thought that they were siblings or perhaps cousins. He did not know why he thought this except they were always together and moved through the town in a way that seemed as if they had been in each other's life for a very long time.

In the town they were known as the beggar children, as all of them were, the young ones here who made their homes in the alleyways or in the settlement not far from the plantation house.

Most of the townspeople ignored them. The children preferred it this way. It was something they understood, and had been shaped by, their world entirely different from the communities already established in this town, in the docks, in the neighborhoods, the shops.

The girl was named Bia.

The boy was called Santi by those who knew him because he had been found at the church and spent his first years there, raised by Peixe. The groundskeeper would wrap the boy in a blanket, strap him onto his back, and work in the garden.

Even when Santi was older and no longer living there, he visited. And the two of them spent the night outdoors, Peixe setting out an extra plate for him, still cutting his food, and Santi allowing it.

He was small for his age. He wanted to be a sailor, though he had never learned to swim. Still, on most mornings and evenings he could be seen on the coast, watching the boats leave and return.

Santi was probably eight years old. Bia was perhaps seven years older. They were unsure of their age but seemed unbothered by it.

Some days Yohan met them by chance in the alleyways. At first they fled into the shadows or stood there caught in nervousness. But soon they grew used to him and he helped them search the trash bins, sifting through the bags to find objects they could keep or use to trade with the others: a comb, a picture frame, a pair of leather shoes Santi tried on, grinning, too large for him but clean and stylish.

Bia wrapped a handkerchief around him and he pretended it was a necktie. He wore the handkerchief and the shoes for days, walking along the beaches toward the settlement, pleased with himself and humming a song he had heard on the radio station.

The next time Yohan saw them they appeared with bruises on their faces and their arms. The boy was barefoot, the shoes and the handkerchief gone. They refused to meet Yohan's eyes, both of them unwilling to speak of it. Buttons were missing on both of their shirts. Bia gathered her hair in her hands so that Kiyoshi could clean a scratch on her neck. They spent the afternoon in the alley beside the shop, avoiding the stares of the passersby while the tailor mended their clothes.

They did not visit the shop often. When they did, it was when it was empty and Kiyoshi would clap his hands, hurry across the room, and welcome them. He brought them food and offered them clean shirts and men's trousers, which they rolled up to their shins, these spare clothes he had made or clothes that were abandoned by customers who had left the town years ago.

On a high shelf the tailor kept a cigar box where Santi stored the things he collected. Sometimes the boy sat in front of the shop and opened the box and revisited the objects—costume jewelry, a guitar pick, a stone—while Bia circled the narrow street on Kiyoshi's bicycle. On the sidewalk lay some food the tailor had left for them, wrapped in newspaper. The boy would chase her around the street, carrying the foil wrapper of a chocolate bar, which held the sunlight as though his fingertips were on fire.

One time, in the afternoon, Santi came and stood in front of the tailor's dummy. Yohan had been making tea. He parted the curtain. A moment before, Kiyoshi had gone to the market and the boy was alone in the shop.

Santi mouthed some words. He bit his lip. He formed his hands into fists and began to move his feet. Then he struck the dummy in the chest. It creaked and swayed on its pedestal. The noise of it and the dust from its skin filled the room. Then he struck it again. And again. Each time the dummy swayed farther, its shadow swinging across the floor. That heavy sound and the body spitting dust toward the ceiling.

Afterward, in exhaustion, he fell asleep under the dummy, fitting his body into the space and using a roll of fabric as a pillow until Bia came looking for him.

He began to fight with the other boys. They fought in the fields or in the alleyways or on the coast. Fought over food or the things they found. Cuts and scratches appeared on his hands and his face. Bia would grab the boy's arm and yell at him, but on his face was a calm, as if he were not listening to the girl at all but was far away somewhere beyond the hill town.

Yohan did not know why Santi fought and whether or not he started it. He never asked.

Kiyoshi had known them almost all their lives. Around them he moved with eagerness and smiled often.

Years before Yohan came, Kiyoshi was resting in the

meadow one afternoon. When he woke, a child stood above him.

—Hi, the child said. Are you my father?

Kiyoshi, still in a dream, could not speak.

The boy said, —That's okay. Now we're friends.

And he kneeled to hold the tailor's hand for a moment before he left.

Santi used to approach the people of the town, asking them if they were his mother or father, the men and women looking down at him in either confusion or amusement or sadness as he lifted his hand for them to shake. In the port he followed the sailors around while Peixe looked for him in the town.

Once, he and another child had attempted to scale the church spire. The other one fell. Kiyoshi witnessed it. It was early evening. The forms of two children appeared in the sky. The first stars beside them. Then a sound, an exhalation and the clawing of fingernails against stone, and one of them falling. He thought they were ghosts.

He pushed through the crowd that had gathered around the fallen boy. The streetlamps had turned on. The boy was trying to move and Kiyoshi saw between the shadows of those standing that he could not, saw the effort manifested in the child's blinking eyes.

Kiyoshi held him as a doctor cut his trousers. He leaned forward, smoothed the boy's hair. He covered the boy's ears. His eyes now quiet. His snot dripped onto Kiyoshi's wrists. He had fixed his gaze on the knot of the tailor's tie as if he had found something there.

Kiyoshi felt a hand on his back. He turned to find Santi hiding behind him, trembling. He had cut his palm while descending the spire and it stained the tailor's shirt.

The boy lived but did not stay, leaving the town not long after. Kiyoshi would watch as Santi wandered the roads, his hand wrapped in a bandage, asking whether anyone had seen him.

The girl Yohan knew less of. She first appeared at the church looking for food. She helped Peixe with the chores, digging in the garden or cleaning the stained-glass windows or mopping the floors. She helped take care of Santi.

In the end he went with her. And Peixe, not wanting to fight with them, leaned against his cane and followed their departure as thc two children headed toward the coastal road, this seed of restlessness they shared growing through the years.

She often rode Kiyoshi's bicycle. And Yohan saw flashes of her, the length of her bright hair and the bicycle wheels between buildings, a reflection caught in a window. If there was music playing in the town, she searched for it, staying on the periphery of a crowd. Other times, in passing, he saw her sitting in an alley beside the narrow window of a basement music club. She leaned against the wall with her legs crossed. She hummed along with the musicians as she shut her eyes and swayed.

There were days when she would cling to Santi, her small hands wrapped around him as she pressed him against her. Sometimes she slept under the tree in the late afternoons, curled against the trunk as though she had arrived from a very long journey, a line of sweat following the curve of her spine.

Her skin was the color of the tiled rooftops.

He liked the way she said his name. In the town he did not hear it often. It sounded different from the way Kiyoshi said it or even the way he had heard it over the years. She said it with patience, taking her time, briefly holding each syllable before letting go.

—Yohan, she called from across the market or as she passed the shop, her hand in the air and a few people turning to look.

5

They became a part of his days, Santi and Bia, just as their coming and going did. During some months he did not see them for weeks. Then they suddenly appeared in the town as if they had never left.

Yohan kept busy at the shop, measuring the men for their new suits, making alterations and adjustments. He now knew who wore what. When they came for their clothes he was able to hand them over before they spoke. He knew most of the neighborhoods now, knew the names of the streets, and he continued to make deliveries.

He grew more familiar with the language. He began

to converse with the market vendors, asking them about the fish and the fruit they sold. He ran errands for Kiyoshi, stepping out to the pharmacy to purchase soap or to a Japanese restaurant to pick up dinner.

Every few weeks he and Kiyoshi went to an Italian barber whom the tailor had known for years. Kiyoshi would never get a haircut. Instead he sat in the corner and exchanged town gossip with the man while Yohan's hair was trimmed and he was given a shave.

They spoke in Portuguese and he listened as they discussed the ongoing love affair between a waitress and a dockworker. There was also the woman with a pet bird who had a habit of talking to her dead husband when she believed no one could hear. A boardinghouse near the port was in fact a brothel.

Later, taking a walk, he asked Kiyoshi about the words he had not understood, and the tailor translated them for him in Japanese, grinning.

In the winter of 1956, a week of cold weather began. They kept their windows closed, Yohan's body no longer used to it. He and Kiyoshi wore sweaters. He had not worn one since the war. It took him a day to grow accustomed to the weight on his shoulders and his arms.

Neighbors brought in coats they had long ago placed in storage, asking for a new lining, a new button.

One afternoon it took effort for Kiyoshi to rise from his chair. All that morning he had paused in his work and stared at his hands.

He retired early and remained in his room. That evening when Yohan brought him tea he saw the man lying there with his arms raised toward the ceiling. He continued to stare at his hands. It was as though they were not his at all, as though he no longer recognized them.

—It's all right, the old man said. It's just a cold. I'll sleep for a little while.

Yohan called the doctor. He was young and dressed in one of Kiyoshi's suits. Through the space in the curtains Yohan could see him sitting beside Kiyoshi's bed, a stethoscope placed against the tailor's chest.

—There's nothing wrong with him, he told Yohan later, the two of them standing in the shop.

After he left, Kiyoshi sat down at his table and began to work. Then he paused and lifted his head, staring at the wall in front of him.

He said, —You didn't need to do that, and returned to the shirt he was mending.

Whatever it was gradually left him, day by day, though there were remnants: he slept more, waking up later. It was Yohan who opened the shop now. And although the old man continued to care for his customers and measure them without delay, it took him longer to complete an article of clothing.

On a Sunday when the shop was closed, Yohan spent an afternoon at the harbor. It was quieter than the other days. There was the occasional whistle of a machine. The sound of bottles and ice being spread over fish. He passed stacks of empty crates. He looked up at the vessels in the sunlight, scanning the names on the bows in all the various languages until he arrived at the last pier to the south.

He heard his name. A short man with a graying beard waved and approached him. They stood facing each other and the man laughed, admiring Yohan's sweater.

—Wanting to go back out onto the water? the sailor said.

They embraced. A year had passed since they had last seen each other. He was startled by how much the man had aged: the wrinkles around his eyes, his thinning hair, the slight stoop as he walked.

—It's just me now, the sailor said, pointing at the

crew who was beginning to unload the vessel's cargo, all of whom Yohan had never seen before.

They spoke Korean. He had not heard or spoken it in a year. It took him a moment to find certain words.

One of the men had died, a crane accident. The rest had changed jobs and crews, moving to other routes and crossing the Pacific toward the western United States.

He patted Yohan on the shoulder.

—But you, he said. You will stay.

And he laughed again and looked back toward the ship where a man was sliding crates down a plank.

—Ah, he said. Yours.

They moved down the pier where there were two shipments of textiles from Tokyo and Osaka. He did not leave right away. He sat on one of the crates, facing the sea, and the sailor sat on the other. The water was blue and gray and broke as the birds dove.

The sailor had been living on the southern coast of Japan all these years, joining a cousin, a migrant worker who had gone there before the war. The sailor had two sons and a daughter. His wife, a Japanese woman, worked at a hotel now, washing linen.

—It's new, he said. The hotel. It's ruined her hands.

He raised his palms in the air.

He did not see her often. They exchanged letters when they could, the wife writing to his next destination. Sometimes, when she knew he would be stopping in Brazil, she sent a letter to Yohan's shop because he had offered.

He would carry it to the docks and the sailor would read the letter aloud to Yohan, who imagined the small house in the coastal village: how each day the sailor's wife followed the road down to the beach where the hotel stood. She carried a lunch box and a parasol for shade. The children went to school and then returned home to his wife's mother. Some days the hotel was empty but still she cleaned the rooms and made the beds. Lifting sheets the color of ivory and that color everywhere. A thousand empty tents.

But a letter had not come to the shop this time. He did not have to tell the sailor, who knew already because Yohan had not given him anything.

—I will see them soon, he said, and watched a small boat leave the harbor.

When he did not go on, Yohan looked at him, searching the man's eyes, and waited.

The sailor said, —Nothing. I have not heard news of your town.

He did not say anything more. Yohan knew what he meant. He stayed a while longer but they did not speak much, as though they had both said what they needed to say. The sailor mentioned Korea, about the southeastern port that he docked at, the one from which Yohan had embarked, but that was all.

He wondered how different that port looked now, whether there were new buildings and new ships, whether it was busier, but he did not ask. He shivered; he wrapped his arms around his stomach. He had once stood in the cold among ships that were like towers. Then the Americans escorting him pointed to a distant vessel where silhouettes moved across the high deck under a sky of long clouds.

How long ago that was now. How long ago was his own exhaustion and the exhaustion of the men escorting him, their bloodshot eyes and their helmets and the reek of iodine and gunpowder that they all carried and seemed to take years to erase. There were days even now when he could still smell it, and that evening on the coast did not seem so far away then.

For a moment, he was still that man, a boy, in that country, in that harbor, with his back to the years that had happened and unsure of whether those years would follow him into the sea. He remembered the uncontrollable shaking of his body. The pause on the gangplank and himself above the water as though suspended between the coast and the ship.

He remembered the sailor standing beside him as they entered the harbor here that early morning. He had lit a cigarette and the two of them watched as the other ships unloaded their cargo and the peddlers walked back and forth along the docks, carrying boxes strapped over their necks, selling stationery and pornography.

—Yohan, the sailor had said. Stay here. Stay for a long time.

The day dimmed and the dock lights flared. In the distance, beyond the piers, he recognized Kiyoshi's bicycle and then Bia riding it. She circled the market square, bumping over the cobblestone, and then pedaled past the crates and the men. A scarf covered her hair. Santi was seated on the bicycle, holding her waist.

The bike tottered and for a moment it seemed as though Bia was on the verge of losing her balance. Yohan found himself standing. But she regained control and continued on, laughing. Dockworkers shook their heads and then returned to their work.

Whether they saw him he could not tell.

—They've grown, the sailor said.

Santi leaned back, his legs in the air as she pedaled past the men and headed toward the boardwalk. When they lost her in a far crowd, Yohan offered the sailor a room to spend the night, as he always did, but the sailor refused, as he always did.

—Next time, the sailor said, and they parted ways, Yohan pushing the crates up the hill on a dolly, and the sailor returning to the ship, to his cabin, where there was a narrow bed, photographs, his wife's letters, a ceramic dolphin his children had given him, two coins a shipmate once placed on his pillow, years ago.

6

From his window that evening he saw the shape of someone riding a bicycle through the town. There was a flashlight on the handlebars and he followed the errant star as it swayed down the slope and faded along the coast.

He left the shop. He passed the church and entered the meadow. He continued to walk away from the town, moving under the open sky, until the land narrowed and formed a promontory high above the sea. He took the path beside it, descending the cliff.

The brightness of the low moon was everywhere. For a moment he was disoriented. He squinted, shielding his eyes with a hand. He was on a beach north of the harbor, the sand gleaming and unbroken. The shadow of an animal, a dog perhaps, retreated into a thicket. A piece of torn paper twirled past him.

In the distance, farther up the beach, a fire was burning. He could distinguish the silhouettes of people in the darkness: some were sitting with blankets over their shoulders; others were standing. A girl lifted her arms and stretched, her body a blade against the light of the fire, a leaping fish.

He felt the softness of the sand, its give. The water blinked from the nearby lighthouse as he moved along the shoreline. He heard conversations. The calm of the night hours.

He kept walking. He found the old plantation house on the coast. It stood in a long field, beyond a stone wall. In the evening light it looked as if it had just been built. But as he approached he noticed its dilapidated architecture, the wood-covered windows, the sinking porch, a portion of its rooftop gone.

Nearby, shanties stood in rows. They were short and squat with steel roofs that reflected the evening light. Some of them were without windows. Others had the space for a door but there was none, the entrances covered in heavy blankets.

A path had been made among them and in the moonlight he watched a man on a mule pace through the settlement. Two women carried baskets into a shanty. At one entrance a pair of gray dogs lay side by side with their heads on their paws. A group of old men, with their hats hooked over their knees, smoked cigarettes.

There was also a large tree in the field. Clothes of various colors hung on its branches, left to dry. Bia was standing under it. She was wearing a hat pulled low over her eyes. She unfurled a shirt and threw it over a branch.

He climbed over the stone wall. Water hit the hulls of the small boats lined up along the shore. He could hear himself breathing, hear the beats of his heart starting to speed and then slow as he moved away from the beach and entered the settlement. It was as though someone, somewhere, were dreaming this and he had crossed into it without permission. Everything both familiar and foreign.

A man on crutches walked past, nodding. A basket of dried fish was tied to his waist. Across the field, closer to the plantation house, he saw the figure of a juggler, his chin pointing at the sky. A group of children, sitting around him, were following his motions.

Bia did not seem surprised to see him. He looked up at the clothes hanging above them in the tree, these shapes in the air like windows afloat. A house of fabric. Drops of water hit his wrist.

Without speaking she led him away toward the plantation house. The man on the mule greeted her and as they passed she patted the animal on the neck. She spoke briefly with a girl, leaving her a folded shirt.

Santi was sitting on a large blanket, watching them. Around him lay the bracelets, necklaces, and the long coiled rope they had woven. In the morning they would bring them to the market. They would sit all day, selling what they could.

Not far from them the children had gathered in a circle. They were leaning back and clutching the grass. Some wore sweaters and others wore wool caps. Many of them were barefoot.

The juggler stood at the center, throwing the children's shoes into the air. He had a faded red scarf wrapped around his eyes. His shoulders were narrow and he wore a loose shirt that revealed his collarbones. His arms moved like wheels, without pause. The ends of his scarf swayed. His blinded face tilted toward the night clouds.

Santi made room for them. In the moonlight a bruise revealed itself on his cheek. Yohan pretended not to notice. Instead he unwrapped a chocolate bar and shared it with them.

He could feel the wet grass against his palms. The cool of the blanket on his ankles. He looked back toward the settlement. On the rooftop of a shanty stood a cluster of potted plants. From the ground a cat jumped the height and began to claw at the leaves. Someone was playing a French song on a gramophone.

He did not know what time it was. It could have been midnight or even later. The night was clear and fell on the land. On occasion a car could be heard; but from here the town was invisible, blocked by headlands and cliffs.

Yohan had tasted chocolates for the first time at the camp. They had been sent from America. A nurse rested the bar on the damp operating table, then cut it with a surgeon's knife.

She shared it with those in the field tent. Pieces the size of fingernails. He stood in the corner and placed a piece on his tongue and kept his lips pressed together, unused to the flavor, the sweetness. Watching the men on the cots and the other nurses do the same. All of them silent as though they each held a secret.

The nurse had also given some to a boy who lived beyond the camp. In the days that followed Yohan would see him through the fences, standing in the fields, looking down at his shirt where there was a chocolate stain, which he licked. When the taste vanished he continued to lift the spot on his shirt and sniff. He did so long after the scent faded. Each time he grinned. Then he moved on to wherever he was going, heading into the woods with a kite strapped to his back.

In the field, shoes rose high and descended. Up and down they went. There was applause and laughter. He heard the coast. Then a ship's horn blew. The lights of a long vessel appeared at sea. It moved so slowly that he was not sure it was moving at all.

Santi reached for another piece of chocolate and then he was gone, running across the settlement toward the beach. In the dark his body was barely visible. He found a high rock and from there he lifted his hands to form an imaginary spyglass, which he swiveled out toward the blinking lights of the vessel.

—They work on the farms and in the mines, Bia said,

looking out at the settlement and the beach fire. There are also fishermen and factory workers.

Then she took his hand and smoothed his palm. She placed his hand on her lap, looked down, studied it. He saw a clarity in her eyes. With her index finger she traced the line that curved around the base of his thumb. The warmth of her skin surprised him.

—You are going to live for a very long time, she said. There's a split, however. You will come upon a great obstacle. You will go around it, see, where it forks near your wrist. It is your character. To go around. For a moment, here—she tapped his skin—you will live a different life.

She spoke slowly so that he would understand. It was the first time she had spoken more than a few words to him. It seemed that she had described both a life sometime in the future and one he had already lived.

He wanted her to go on, wanted her to continue speaking, to be surrounded by her voice, but she raised her eyes and he looked up to see the juggler leaning over them with a curious expression.

Then the juggler frowned and tightened his mouth, brought a finger to his lips, and snatched Bia's hat. All this while still blindfolded and without dropping a single thing.

Bia, blushing, dropped Yohan's hand. They both returned to watching the blindfolded juggler, who was now walking in circles with the shoes and the hat aloft, sometimes running and bending his body.

The children cheered. An airplane appeared behind the mountain range. Clothes were collected from the tree and some more were placed there. Smoke from the fire rose above the field.

The night grew colder. He watched the girl's hat rise and fall, its brim spinning in the air.

Santi was still standing on the high rock. Yohan followed the boy's gaze out toward the blinking water. He waited, though what he was waiting for he was no longer sure of. His legs grew heavy, he felt his palms settle into the grass, and he imagined himself sinking, his body falling into the earth until the sea claimed him and there was nothing left, no evidence of him.

He wondered who would notice his vanishing, who would miss him then.

He watched the ends of the scarf swing behind the blindfolded juggler. He thought of forests. High canopies. A river. A hand on his elbow. Peng.

He thought of new towns in the places he had been. New houses. New shops. Bicycles. Markets. Magic shows, theater, and children.

Bia's hat rose into the air.

Before he left that night she leaned toward him so that their faces were almost touching. He felt her breath against his ear.

She cupped her mouth and said, —He practices every afternoon. To keep him sharp. He used to be in the circus. Then he went to the war. And now he is blind. But he can still throw and catch. He tells me he does not need his eyes for this. He tells me, when he performs, everyone assumes he can see. So he wraps a scarf over his face and they are thrilled. He prefers it that way. The belief that he can see even when the show finishes and the audience has gone. He wants me to imagine this. It makes him happy. So that when we part today, I go this way and he goes that way. He enters his home and unties the scarf around his head and looks around and out the window. He rubs his eyes, squints from the light. I imagine this for him. In my dreams he takes all of us by the waist and throws us into the air. He lifts his arms and we rise. He watches us. And it is beautiful.

7

He had once played cards with the medics. He had been looking for Peng, wondering where he had wandered off to. It was the first summer, an early evening, and no one could sleep.

In one of the hospital tents, three men had gathered around a wooden crate. Peng was there. They were sitting together with their shirts unbuttoned, surrounded by candles, the small fires catching the mosquitoes.

They motioned for Yohan. So he went under the tent and sat on one of the crates beside them. He watched them finish their game.

Then someone asked if he and Peng wanted to play,

too. The game was called poker, they said, and one of the medics taught them the suits.

Peng held the playing cards. The bandages over his eyes were illuminated. When it was their turn he waited for Yohan to whisper into his ear what he held, the numbers and the shapes, the clovers and the portraits of kings.

They did not play very well. They took too long and did not understand the game.

Even so, in that candlelight, Peng clutched the cards and smiled. It was one of the few times Peng smiled at the camp and Yohan would remember it, wondering what private memory he was reliving on that summer night, behind the bandages; what moment or story there was for him in a handful of cards and their texture, the way he ran his fingertips over them as though he held something remarkable. As though for a brief instant, life in this prison camp, near the southern coast of this country, during wartime, had become a kind of wonder.

Just as Yohan would sit with Santi and Bia one day in the market square, the three of them playing cards as they tried to sell bracelets and necklaces. How he paused, holding a three of diamonds, thinking of this night.

Later, he and Peng were split up and Yohan looked over the shoulder of the medic named Lamont. Lamont asked which cards he should give up and Yohan pointed at one and the medic frowned and shook his head.

Lamont had very pale hair that was curly and thick and he had freckles on his nose.

—Snowmen, they called Yohan and Peng, because the Americans knew who they were.

They had found them in the mountains, not far from the wreckage of a bomb, lying buried in the snow. They had found them because Yohan's nose had been sticking up in the snow.

—Like a fucking carrot, they said.

And they had speared his nose with the butt of a rifle, assuming if he were alive, he would react. That sudden sound of bone cracking the air and Yohan screaming.

He had been part of a patrol unit in the mountains that day. Among the men he and Peng had lived with, walked with, fought and slept beside, they were the only survivors of the bombing.

He would not know how many days passed. He would wake momentarily to his body shaking on the bed of a truck, his wrists bound, a warmth spreading across his face, then the pain.

And Peng beside him, his eyes already gone.

The medics were all his age. He remembered being

envious of their boots and the sound of the sleeping convalescents and the nurses pausing to view the card game.

Two of the medics left that month. He did not know where they went. Or whether they lived. They each carried a large pack on their shoulders, heading toward the gate where a transport was waiting. They walked like old men, using their rifles as canes.

—Snowman, they called to him, and waved from the fences.

They had left their gramophone for the nurses. Benny Goodman filled the days and the nights.

When it grew cold the wounded were moved into the abandoned mill. That December, boxes arrived filled with streamers, lights, and hats in the shape of cones.

Lamont, the medic who stayed, walked by the beds, passing out the hats.

—Yohan, a nurse called one late evening, swaying from the whiskey that had been sent as well.

—Dance with me, she said.

It was Christmas. Wood stoves burned on each end of the factory floor. She took his hand and led him outside. It had snowed and their boots dipped into it. All across the field the snow was lit from the brightness of electricity.

They stood under a window so that they could hear the music. She had put on one of the hats, blue in color, and it sparkled. She put one on him as well. He had never danced before.

She took his hands and placed them around her waist. Then she wrapped her arms around his neck and stepped to the side, humming, and he followed her. She smelled of liquor and tiredness. She was wearing her uniform. Yohan wore a coat they had given him.

Behind the factory windows a pastor read to the men. Missionaries carried trays of hot chocolate. A range of pointed colored hats appeared against the fogged glass. A few guards stood looking down at them. Her hat slid off as she rested her head against his chest and they danced in that field in the snow.

All those days there was music. He could hear it as he waited for his meals or washed clothes. As he walked along the perimeter for exercise, Peng holding his elbow and counting steps. As he watched the doctors bend over the cots and as trucks arrived with more of the wounded. As he learned how to mend clothes. As he was taught how to garden. As he stood far in the field and dug into the earth, taking turns with the six available shovels while the others used pickaxes or buckets or even their hands, moving down the fresh slope. Their shoulders heaved. From across the distance men watched from their beds. And that faint melody, a song, came to them as the nurse he had danced with, that winter, lit a lantern and reached over the graves as it grew dark.

8

One night there was a power outage in the town. They headed to the rooftop. Kiyoshi carried a flashlight. They sat in their chairs and the tailor pointed the beam out toward the buildings. Birds had gathered on clotheslines and television antennas. There were no clouds. Everywhere candles began to fill the windows.

There was a quiet in the evening, as if the electricity had taken sound with it. The beam of the lighthouse swept across the water. Musicians began to play in the square near the port and they listened to the melodies traveling up the hill.

Their eyes adjusted to the dark. Even though it was warm Kiyoshi was wearing a sweater.

—I've spent my life looking down and away, the tailor said, spreading his arms to form his imaginary worktable. I have not looked up enough.

He leaned back against his chair and lifted his head.

—What stars, he said, and laughed, gazing up at that vast canvas above them, Yohan astonished by how it was possible that it was the same sky through all their years, in countries across the sea. How the sky never changed, never appeared to grow old.

From below came the rapid patter of footsteps. A trail of lights moved in the dark. When it grew closer he saw that it was a group of boys and girls, out past their curfew, heading down toward the harbor square.

He wondered what it was about the dark of a town that made some stay indoors and others leave their homes, running through the narrow streets in sudden happiness. As if it were not the town they moved through but somewhere in their imaginations, their private castles.

He did not know where Santi and Bia were this evening. He did not know if they always stayed in the settlement when they were here.

—All over, Kiyoshi had said when he asked.

Kiyoshi had offered the shop to them once but they shook their heads, hurrying away with the food he gave them. In the war Yohan had seen a child asleep under a tree with a sack filled with food tied around his wrist. Their footsteps woke him and the child reached for the sack first, then sat up, rubbed his eyes, looked at them, and yawned.

The line of lights faded down the hill. Kiyoshi tugged on Yohan's shirtsleeve.

—Look, he said, and pointed toward the sea.

Another light had appeared, a red star in the water. It was heading north. It was too dark, too far for them to see the shape of the vessel. Soon it vanished behind a building in front of them.

In that moment Kiyoshi said, —Oh, and Yohan felt his arm brush against his, the arrival of a night wind, and the tailor was gone.

At first he did not understand where Kiyoshi was. He looked back at the rooftop door but it was shut. Then he rushed to the rooftop's edge.

But he stopped. In his periphery he caught a flash of movement, the movement of erratic light in the air. He turned toward the rooftops beside theirs, up the slope of the hill, and he saw him there, two buildings away, his figure like some bird tiptoeing along the edge of the concrete and the tiles, across roofs that were flat and some that were pitched, the flashlight swinging beside him and illuminating his ankles.

He called to Kiyoshi several times, but by then the tailor was too far and could not hear him or was ignoring him.

And so Yohan crossed the roof and stepped onto the edge of his neighbors'. He moved as fast as he could, extending his arms to the side and following the beam of the flashlight. It seemed to him that Kiyoshi moved faster, with an energy he had not seen in years, the man running, almost, accompanied by the sound of tiles shifting.

Kiyoshi did not stop until he reached the last building before the church. If the old man was tired, he did not show it. The roof was flat and Yohan kneeled to rest, waiting for the pulsing in his legs to calm.

From where they stood, not far from the church spire, they could see the entire coast. On a cliff the lighthouse stood against the sky, not functioning.

—No light, Kiyoshi said.

He raised his flashlight and began to turn it on and off.

Soon the vessel appeared, drifting past the town. Kiyoshi swayed his arm. He continued clicking the flashlight on and off. In moments like these the lighthouse keeper hung lanterns, and Yohan could see them now and he wondered if Kiyoshi did, too.

He said, —Kiyoshi, it's all right, and touched his shoulder but the tailor did not respond. The ship had passed safely and was far away now.

In the building across from them, in the floor below, a window was open. Candles illuminated the room. He caught the corner of a robe and then a woman appeared. Her gray hair, blond in the candlelight, touched her waist.

A birdcage stood in the corner of the room. She approached it and leaned forward. She spoke and the bird twisted its head. Then she placed a blanket over the cage and Yohan watched as she stood there for some time, holding a hairbrush, staring at the draped fabric, her expression vague and the candlelight shifting across the room from a wind.

The lighthouse returned, its generators humming as the beam flashed across the water. Kiyoshi lowered his arm and they stood there, on a stranger's rooftop, looking out at the water as voices from the port reached them and other windows opened.

• • •

As the months went on Kiyoshi began to spend more time in his room. Yohan finished the work in the shop and then brought tea and sat beside him. He lay propped up on a pillow on his cot with a book and a thin blanket draped over him. He had grown thinner, his clothes a bit looser on him. But he was always awake when Yohan came, his energy still there, and they spoke of the day or about the book he was reading.

Yohan did not know why the man preferred his bedroom over the shop now. But he continued to cross the kitchen every evening, bringing tea and conversation. He kept the doorway open so that they could listen to the radio.

He stayed until Kiyoshi fell asleep. He pulled the book away from his fingers and placed it on the nightstand. He tucked Kiyoshi's slippers under the cot. He dusted the suit jacket hanging from a nail on the wall. He watched Kiyoshi's chest rise and fall. A fly landed on the old man's wrist and Yohan swept it away.

The days grew busier. Yohan kept the store hours himself. Soon he worked into the night. He left the shutters open. There was the occasional shadow of a pedestrian or a child's face against the window, looking in.

The neighborhood, and the town, grew accustomed to him alone; they understood that they would now be working with him.

Late one night Yohan was woken by a noise. He thought at first there were mice in the walls. It resembled a faint scratching sound, the movements of tiny bodies. The glow of a shop sign came in from the window. He heard the noise again. He realized it was coming from under the floor, from below. He rose and, as quietly as he could, descended the stairs.

The shop light was on. The shutters over the store windows were closed. Through a space in the curtain he could make out the tailor's dummy in the center of the room.

A coat covered it. It was a child's winter coat. It was made of wool, gray in color, double-breasted with wide lapels and dark buttons, like the ones the sailors wore.

Kiyoshi stood in front of it. Kiyoshi and the dummy were the same height. He was in his undershirt. His hair was tied back and wrapped in a bun and his glasses hung on a string around his neck.

Music came from the radio. He tilted his head and the light reflected the pin he was holding between his lips.

The old man stood still for some time. There were

long shadows on the floor. Then he took the pin from his mouth and reached for the shoulders of the coat. But his hands shook. He calmed them and stepped away. He put on his glasses. He tried again and his hands shook some more but he ignored it and reached for the coat.

Yohan followed the light reflecting against the pin, the way it fell from Kiyoshi's fingers, the bright sliver spinning in the air before it hit the floor.

Kiyoshi kneeled and ran his palms along the wood. And then he began to cry, kneeling there with his head bowed and his shoulders shaking.

In the years to come, Yohan would think often of this night. Why he did not go to him. Why he stayed behind that curtain, watching all this through a narrow space. Why he turned soon after and returned to his room, where he lay on his mattress, unable to sleep.

But before he left a curious thing occurred. Kiyoshi wiped his face. He stood. He rested his head against the shoulders of the child's coat. He shut his eyes and spoke, as though he were praying or confiding in someone, his face buried in an imaginary neck, his words directed at an imaginary ear.

The words were brief. It lasted a moment, no longer.

One evening a week later, the tailor fell asleep while

reading in bed. Yohan lifted the book from Kiyoshi's hands. He left the room, carrying the tea he had brought.

Kiyoshi never woke. Yohan found him in the morning. He stood in the doorway, waiting, in case he was mistaken. He kneeled. He held the hand hanging over the cot's edge. The hand was riddled with calluses, still warm. He reached for a strand of hair stuck to the old man's lips and pulled it away.

He could hear his own breathing. The sound of the shop's ceiling fan. The quiet static of an empty radio station. The echo of someone passing through the street. Then the teakettle whistled.

Kiyoshi was buried in the cemetery behind the church. Peixe dug the grave. All of his customers came. On the high ridge, under the tree, Yohan saw Santi and Bia looking down over the church walls.

He stayed in his room for the rest of that day. He approached the window, waiting for Santi and Bia to come, but they didn't. He leaned against the wall and thought of this man whom he did not know but without whom he could not imagine the three years that had already passed. He thought of their days in the shop and their evenings on the rooftop and their shared, quiet laughter. He thought of the tailor's kindness and felt it still.

In the corner stood the umbrella that was given to him a long time ago. He tilted it away from the wall until it found the window light, and he held it there, reminding himself to mend the tear in the blue canopy.

In the days that followed, Yohan slept less. As it grew dark he avoided his room and even the shop.

He took walks through the town. Some nights he visited the piers where dockworkers loaded cargo onto a ship. He listened to the musicians in the square. He watched couples sitting at outdoor tables under bright awnings. He looked into the windows of stores. He smelled the fleeting scent of torn fruit in a street gutter.

He moved through the alleyways, closing his eyes and navigating the dark with his hands against the brick walls. He found a small wooden handle to something, a magnifying glass or some child's toy. He found a box of pencils. A model railroad car the length of his palm. He slipped them into his pockets.

Late one evening he was returning to the shop when he saw the door open. Night filled the room as he entered.

A shelf was broken, a vase shattered. Rolls of fabric

had tipped over and unraveled. The tailor's dummy lay on the floor, a single cut down its chest, revealing tufts of gray.

He heard a noise and turned. In a corner shadow he saw the form of a man's body. And then the man leapt and rushed at him, heading for the door, and Yohan stumbled and fell. He grasped at the man's ankles. A forgotten stone turned within him. He lurched forward, grabbing the man's shoulders. He pushed him against the door. He heard the drum of skin against glass and he threw him onto the ground.

Yohan moved on top of him. His hand formed into a fist. He pulled the thief's head back and his throat shone and his lips parted like a fish's. He saw now the face lying below him, unmoving in that light, and he saw that it was not a man but a boy, and Yohan heard his name.

He heard the boy say, —Leave me alone.

And, as if surfacing from water, he felt his body let go. The shop and the night noises from the streets returned to him. He attempted to stand but he couldn't, the energy had left him, and he leaned back against the leg of a table and looked across at Santi on the ground.

The boy was lying beside the door. His shirt had torn and his nose was bleeding. Around him lay scattered the things he had collected throughout the years and which Kiyoshi kept for him.

Santi sat up and began to gather the objects: a comb, a toothbrush, shoelaces, a pocket mirror. The lid of the cigar box was broken. Still he gathered whatever he could, kneeling there and placing them in the box.

Then he stopped. He looked around at the shop, at this room that belonged to a man he had known since he was a child. He looked at the ruined dummy, the fallen rolls of fabrics, the scattered pieces of a vase reflecting light.

—It's all junk, Santi said, and he kept repeating those words, —It's all junk, and he sunk to the ground and covered his face with his hands.

Yohan moved toward him. He stood. He lifted the boy, and the boy let him. He felt Santi's thin arms around his neck. He felt the boy's breathing slow. Smelled the sea on him. He stepped closer to the window and looked out and held him.

9

He did not see Santi for a long time afterward. He did not see Bia either. He took over the tailor's shop. He worked in the mornings and the evenings and delivered clothes in the afternoons. He remained on the second floor and left Kiyoshi's bedroom as it was. He kept the radio on. The shop thrived.

One afternoon he visited the church. The church bells were ringing through the town. He had finished mending a jacket belonging to Peixe. The stitching on the shoulders had been torn, the fabric long faded and discolored by the sun and the garden. He had folded the jacket, wrapped it in paper, and bound it with a piece of twine.

It was warmer than other days. The daylight bright against the buildings. A neighbor was washing the sidewalk in front of a store and the water sped down the cobblestone. As he climbed the hill a motorbike passed him, carrying an open crate of fish lying on their sides. Now and then someone waved or smiled and he returned their gestures.

In the church courtyard an old car was parked in the shade of a tree. There was also a bicycle leaning against the building, under a stained-glass window. The building's walls were whitewashed, its heavy wooden doors the color of clay.

A stone wall surrounded the property and sometimes, after the church emptied, Bia and Santi would sit there and wait for Peixe to appear. And they would stay for a little while with the man who had known them the longest, sitting under the tree or helping him with the chores.

Yohan passed through the front gate. He walked around the side of the building, following a narrow stone path, ducking under the low branches and heading toward the back garden.

There, a brick cottage stood against the slope under the town's ridge. It had once been a gardener's shed, which had been expanded and converted into a living space, a single room with low eaves and four windows, one on each wall. A wheelbarrow rested against one of the walls, as well as empty flowerpots stacked on top of each other.

The path led to the door. He knocked and stepped away. Under the trees there was a silence. He turned to look out at the garden, the rows of vegetables. Vines climbed the back of the church. Farther in the distance lay the headstones, the statues, and the small monuments of the cemetery.

He heard movement from inside the cottage. The door opened and Peixe stood within the doorframe, leaning against his cane and wearing trousers with suspenders over his shirt. A pair of reading glasses was tucked in his shirt pocket. He was taller than Yohan and thin. He had rolled up his sleeves and, like, Kiyoshi, his fingertips were stained by tobacco. He took Yohan's hand and smiled.

—*Alfaiate,* he said, as he always did, greeting Yohan in that way, by his profession.

Yohan handed him the package. Behind the groundskeeper, daylight had found a corner of the one-room cottage. There was a single bureau, a chair, a bed, a small table with a half-eaten meal. A spyglass lay on a shelf.

He invited Yohan inside but then looked out at the day and changed his mind.

—Ah, Peixe said. Yes. It's better outside.

He left the door open, holding the package under his arm the way Yohan had done. Kiyoshi had started the jacket and he did not know whether further alterations would be necessary.

Yohan asked Peixe to try it on but the groundskeeper waved his hand, ignoring him.

They stood on the path and faced the garden, Yohan looking over at a spot where two old tires lay on the ground, filled with fresh soil.

—I found them on the beach, he said. It would have been a waste.

Yohan nodded, imagining Peixe carrying the tires up the hill, his arms hooked through the holes.

—You understand that, no? Peixe said.

He hesitated, unsure what the groundskeeper had asked, and what to say, but before he could respond, Peixe said, —Kiyoshi.

In his eyes there was a kindness and a concern.

—You'd like to visit him, yes?

Yohan remained silent. He looked across at the headstones, searching for the tailor's. There had been little money saved. The church had paid for it.

On the wall inside the cottage he noticed a photograph. He recognized the old plantation house near the coast. In front of it stood a group of men and women and children. They were all Japanese except the two at the side of the photo, a slim woman and a small boy who leaned against a cane.

Peixe brought the photo out to him. With his thumb he wiped away the dust on the glass. He told him that after the landowner died and the house was abandoned, the property had been turned into a hospital for the mountain villages and for the factory workers who had been the victims of mechanical accidents.

It had also been a sanatorium for survivors of polio, he said, and tapped his cane.

—Then, he said, it became part of an internment camp during the Second World War.

He pointed at the people.

—For the Japanese, he said. Those shanties you see now were built then.

—A single place. One house. One piece of land. All the changes. All the lives it once held, however briefly.

The good that was there. Also, the discrimination. It is astonishing, yes?

The plantation house was no longer recognizable. But it was the people in the photograph who seemed far more different, the style of their clothes and something else he could not articulate. Their postures, their stillness. Or perhaps it was knowing that they were no longer of the age when the photographs were taken. That the moment had already gone by the time their images were captured. That people aged, second by second, leaving themselves behind.

He had never been photographed before. He did not know what he would look like, did not know how he would appear on those small pale squares people held and framed and shared.

He had once witnessed a young American wake from surgery and rise from his bed too quickly. His eyes, like Peng's, were wrapped in bandages and, disoriented, he knocked a tray from a nurse's hand. The iodine in the flying bottle stained the convalescent's gauze and he screamed, flailed his arms, feeling that sudden wetness, pleading, —Not again. Please God, not again, as his body shook and his mouth twisted and in his blindness a dream returned to him of the land mine.

Yohan remembered the guard leaning against a tent pole, laughing. And he remembered he could not watch and he turned away, concentrating on the pile of clothes he had been mending, and he remembered the shame of that turning, of looking away. And he remembered the sound of that weeping soldier meeting the sound of the guard's laughter and a doctor shouted, —Shut up, until the guard did not find it funny anymore and grew silent. Then there was just the convalescent, rocking his body and clutching his hands, his face like a ruined painting.

Yohan continued to study the photo. He scanned the faces. He paused at the man toward the end. He was thin and had strong cheekbones and thick eyebrows. His hair was short.

—Yes, Peixe said. Our tailor.

—He was in the Second World War, he continued. But you know this, yes? He was a physician. An army medic in Russia. The Far East. For Japan. I was young when he came. Defectors, the town called them. I saw the high fences being built. The soldiers. The families that were brought here by ship or by trucks. There were so many of them.

—My mother and I used to visit them. I would follow her along the coastal road and wait by the gates as the men checked her bag. Then we were inside and soon people appeared from the shanties and the cabins. You see, she was a schoolteacher. She taught them the language, read to them, brought food. Kiyoshi was very young then. I remember his patience and his gentleness. The way he brought his ear toward me and adjusted his glasses when I wanted to speak. The way he clasped his hands together and circled his thumbs as he listened.

—There was a table there out in the field. On clear days the sun would hit the top and I could see dark stains, from blood, and I grew afraid and would not enter the camp. I thought the soldiers cut the men. And the women and the children. It was Kiyoshi who pointed at the fish they caught, bringing them to the table and even cooking one for me. He was patient. He never hurried. As though he had been to as many places as he ever needed to and that there were no more surprises.

Yohan looked away, his gaze moving across the garden until it focused on the vines on the church wall, crossing over one another and rising toward the eaves.

He asked if there had been a family. Peixe shook his head. He did not know. If there was, the tailor never spoke of them.

—He used to juggle for us. It's true. He would tell me

to choose a stone and my mother would choose another one and so on and we watched as the objects moved in a circle just above Kiyoshi's head, then they went higher, and higher, the circle thinning, and his back bending backward in that long field beside the water. You're still in the air, he always said, and it made me laugh.

—I think he wanted to convince my mother and me that he was happy there. That all of them were. All these men and women who had come here to start new lives. It would not happen for years.

—These days I think that Kiyoshi was a little in love with my mother. And that she was a little in love with him. I don't know if this is true. I will never know. And I cannot explain why but it makes me happy imagining this.

He waited for Peixe to go on but he didn't. From the street came the sound of a passing cart.

—Yes, well, Peixe said, and took out his wallet.

When Yohan refused, he sighed.

—Do you think I'm charity? he said, and, —Why?

Peixe did not wait for a response. Instead he slipped the money into Yohan's shirt pocket, thanked him, and waved his hand across the small plot of land.

—One day, he said, you will come help me with this.

—Yes, Yohan said, and the groundskeeper left, leaning against his cane, the paper package still under his arm.

The wind pushed the cottage door back and forth. In the garden, Peixe began to pick weeds, reaching down, and the glasses in his shirt pocket almost fell, catching the low sun in the trees.

10

They were loaded onto the bed of a truck and taken into the surrounding forest. It was the only time he left the borders of the camp. All through the day he felled trees, the guards gathered on a high riverbank above them. They would use the wood to build additional shelters and for fire.

They were given time to rest and they went into the river. Some of them bathed while others sat in the cool water or washed their faces and their necks.

It was their second year at the camp. Yohan immersed himself, holding his breath, feeling the current pass over him. The life of it.

Peng lay beside him. His body submerged, the dirt on the bandages over his eyes began to loosen. They had been holding on to a boulder. Earlier, they had been speaking of the river in Yohan's town, how in the warm seasons they had gone swimming there. All the children did, entire groups of them navigating the slow current and one another as though they were each a ship.

Yohan spoke of that one time a girl surfaced, unmoving, her back to the sky and the delayed confusion and then the shouting.

Peng asked whether Yohan had known who the girl was. Yohan could not remember.

—Was I there? Peng said.

In the water they faced each other for a moment, the two of them holding their breaths and the sun on them and their bodies afloat. Yohan smiled. Then he shut his eyes.

He would never know when Peng let go. Just that when Yohan looked again beside him he was no longer there.

It happened too quickly. On the banks a guard shouted but Peng remained motionless as he caught the current and floated away, moving faster now with the river.

Two guards started to run, following the banks. Peng grew smaller.

He would always wonder whether Peng heard the shouting. Perhaps he had been daydreaming. Perhaps he had fallen asleep. Perhaps he was aware of what was happening and no longer cared.

He was twenty-six years old. This young man whom he had first seen as a boy in front of an audience, on the shoulders of his father, leaping into the sky. Peng, who once sat on a tree stump in the woods, exhausted, his rifle between his legs, the crescent shape of an orange rind in his mouth and his face frozen in a smile.

On that first day at the camp, he had reached into the air and found Yohan's wrist. He asked where they were, what was happening. They were suddenly surrounded by men and a foreign language. A helicopter deafened the morning. Yohan felt the bandaged face against his shoulder. He held Peng's hand as he looked out at a field of barracks and cabins, an old mill and tents, a graveyard and a garden.

That afternoon in the forest there were four rifle shots and the sounds echoed across the river. In the distance, water sprayed into the air.

It was the last he saw of him. In the madness of those seconds, while everyone around him rushed to the high banks, he was unable to move, standing there, his body rooted in the moving water and all the noise like light against him.

He had done nothing. He had held his breath. He had clasped his hands as though in prayer and he had followed the paleness of his friend's skin in the current.

A week after that, while washing a uniform, he tore it and, startled, he looked down at the wrecked fabric in his hands and wept.

He stayed at the camp for almost a year after the war ended. Most of the prisoners had gone. The field hospital remained active, the doctors and the nurses staying, tending to the remaining Americans and the surviving prisoners. By then they had grown accustomed to Yohan and he assisted them, carrying trays of washcloths and dressings, a bucket of water and a ladle.

The guards no longer watched him. He was free to walk the grounds whenever he wanted. He had the cabin to himself in the evenings. He was unused to the silence and the size. He slept where he always did, in the corner. He was given extra blankets if he needed them.

Some nights he stayed outside, watching the field and the distant farmhouse where a single light burned behind a window. Other nights he walked to the mill, played cards with the men.

One day, in a field tent, he brought out a sewing machine from under a table. He began to mend old and torn and discarded clothes. It was no longer necessary. It was something to do. He rubbed his nose, feeling its crookedness, the bump there. He concentrated on the movement of the work. It came naturally to him.

He worked all day, alone in that tent, finding whatever clothes he could. He washed them as well. Then those still stationed there began to approach him, giving him the shirts they wore.

The worst of the winter had passed. The land was gray.

On Yohan's last day he walked to the edge of the camp. He slipped his fingers through the fence. He could hear a peddler's bell somewhere in the mountains. He heard footsteps. He turned to see the medic, Lamont, approaching him.

—Snowman, the medic said, and stood there behind Yohan with curiosity.

There used to be a kite somewhere in the trees. That nameless boy who was given chocolate by a nurse would call to the prisoners, —Hey, mister! and then run the meadow. The ball of twine he held unraveled, the kite aloft over his shoulders.

Almost always the kite tangled itself at the edge of the woods. And the boy, with patience, would climb the tree and they would all watch, the guards, too, as he vanished into the high foliage.

In that moment it seemed that they all held their breaths, wondering where the boy had gone. But then a hand would appear between the leaves and the camp cheered.

He never knew where the boy lived. He stayed for one season, then traveled farther south, he supposed.

The boy was short. He had lost the use of one of his hands. It hung by his side, bent at the wrist, forever in a halfhearted fist. A mine perhaps. Still, he climbed trees with speed and dexterity, using his thighs and his good arm.

In the end the kite tore, suffering its last crash into the trees. The sound of the tear could be heard in the camp. Men paused in their work and turned. They laughed and hollered and clapped.

The boy approached the base of the tree. He placed a hand above his eyes and raised his head. The tip of a tree branch had pierced one of the wings.

Yohan, expecting the boy to climb the tree once more, waited. But he didn't.

In the months that followed, the kite stayed in the tree. It stayed in the weeks of rain and it stayed as leaves began to fall. The paper darkened and changed form. And then the snow dusted it, brightening it once more, and in the nights it shone like a moon in the trees.

Yohan used to look out at it from time to time, like some coast he was waiting for. Then, as the winter deepened, he no longer did.

He searched for it now but couldn't find it. It had been almost three years since he had woken to his wrists bound and his body shaking from the movements of a truck. This man Lamont who was from Virginia peering down at him, grinning and raising his thumbs.

They stood beside the fence. Lamont turned to him as though about to speak. Then, following Yohan's eyes, he looked up.

11

Three months after Kiyoshi's death, Yohan found the child's coat the tailor had been working on. It had been placed in the chest in the corner of the old man's room. It lay with many other clothes. They were clothes of all sizes and had never been worn.

He carried the coat to the shop and lifted it to the light. It was not yet finished. It was missing a lining and buttons and the cuffs needed to be hemmed but he admired the construction of it and its shape.

Whose it was he did not know. He draped it over the tailor's dummy, where it remained visible through the window.

All that week he asked each customer who entered the shop. He asked the people to whom he delivered clothes. He asked them whether they could ask others.

—Are you missing clothes? he said.

They shook their heads. It seemed that it did not belong to anyone. Or at least anyone here in this town.

One afternoon he approached the windows. A group of children had gathered in front of the pastry store. The church bell rung.

Two hours remained before the shop closed; but he turned over the sign on the door. He took the child's coat and laid it over his worktable. He undid the knot of his tie and rolled up his shirt cuffs. He lifted the sewing machine aside.

He worked with patience. He had not worked without the machine in some time. It pleased him to return to it, the work, the movement of his fingers. He lost himself in it.

The day passed and moved into evening. On occasion a shadow appeared: a woman pressed her hand against the window; a man knocked and called to him. He ignored them, increasing the volume on the radio.

When he finished he hung the coat on a rack and sat

looking at it. He saw the shape of the arms and the shoulders as if a child floated there.

He did not know what time it was. Outside, it was dark and the streets empty.

He stood and began to pace the shop. He was not tired. He made himself some tea. He organized the fabrics and rolled the measuring tapes. He climbed the stairs and headed to his room, thinking sleep would come to him if he lay down. Instead he stayed by the window in the dark, looking out at the hill town.

Soon, it began to rain. It fell across the streets and the harbor. He opened the window. The rain hit the tiles of the rooftops, erasing the town noises. He pushed his hand out into the air and felt the cold drops catch his skin.

He was suddenly aware that there was no one else in the house. That there would be no one downstairs when he woke.

He stayed beside the window in his room with its sloped ceiling. He did not sleep. A store sign flickered, throwing its light against the walls of the room. The night passed.

In that hour before dawn he returned downstairs to the shop. He took one of Kiyoshi's leather bags and placed the child's coat in it. He put on a raincoat. In the corner he found Kiyoshi's bicycle. He unlocked the shop door and pushed the bicycle outside.

Though the rain had stopped, the air was now cool. He could smell the wet cobblestone and dirt. Streetlamps were still glowing.

He pushed the bicycle down the street for a while. He hesitated. There was no one. He swung his leg over the seat. He began to pedal slowly, circling the street, passing the tailor's shop a few times. Then he began to pedal faster and when he reached the start of the street he turned.

He went down the slope of the hill, following the roads, going faster now past the shuttered stores and the cafés. He arrived at the port and turned again and when he reached the coastal road he sped.

A field of stars opened above him. The breath of sky. A path of lights on the ocean's surface; and the hill town to his left, all its windows like a blurred image as though another ocean were there, another body of water, draped across the high slope.

The coastal road was empty and bright. He shut his eyes. He leaned back, straightened his legs, and listened to the bicycle wheels. When the bicycle slowed he bent forward and pedaled.

Back and forth he went like this. Toward the settlement, the flashing lighthouse and the northern cities, and then back toward the piers. His chin pointed up, his body stretched against the moonlight. He was smiling.

He could hear the waves pushing toward the coast and he did not want the sound to end. It seemed to him the night would go on, that it would always be dark, the town forever lit by the muted glow of electricity. That it would be a world of nights alone.

He felt a lightness in his chest and breathed the cool air; he could taste it almost, it tasted old and rich as though it had traveled a very long way to reach him, as though he could taste the years it contained. And he felt those years and the land that it had traveled across and the people it had passed; and he thought of how it entered him and how he held it now, within him.

He shut his eyes once more and he thought of others and of times before this one.

He slowed, approaching the settlement. Through the coastal trees he could make out the shanties in the field and the broken rooftop of the plantation house. There were rowboats and canoes in a small bay, bobbing as the water approached and receded. He caught movement in the trees, the thin smoke from a chimney. Fishermen began to appear from the shanties and factory workers headed toward the road.

He stayed a little longer and then he adjusted the bag over his shoulder and returned to the town.

It had become morning, the town the color of a fading fire. A fog was climbing the hill, following him. He was walking, pushing the bicycle up the streets that were still quiet. His breathing was calm as he passed the tailor's shop and continued up the road.

At the church a light had been turned on, illuminating a stained-glass window. He entered the meadow, making his way toward the tree.

There, on that hill, he rested. People began appearing from windows, checking the weather. He could hear the carts heading toward the markets. Behind him, in the fields, mules and cattle were already grazing.

There was just one road that moved across the land, vanishing into the mountains. He had never been to those mountains or beyond them, did not know how far this road extended, whether it continued unbroken through the country.

On a far slope he noticed the shape of someone clothed in white and carrying a basket, picking mushrooms.

He still felt awake. He held his breath and then exhaled. In that moment it seemed as though there was nothing more to know.

When he turned to face the town he saw a figure walking the promontory. He stood under the tree and followed the person's approach. Raindrops fell from the tree onto his raincoat and the mud around him. The fog was thick and the figure slipped in and out of it, heading toward him, growing clearer in the gray light.

It was Bia. She wore a long-brimmed hat and she was carrying a rucksack. She crossed the meadow and climbed the hill. Her boots were stained with mud and the hem of her trousers was wet.

He had not seen her for some time. She stood opposite him, the two of them under the tree. She had tucked her hair under her hat, revealing a pale line around her neck where a necklace had been.

He looked behind her to see if anyone else was coming. A large ship retreated from the harbor.

—He's gone, Bia said. He left.

He asked to where. She shrugged. She didn't know. She adjusted the straps of her rucksack and smiled.

—He'll come back, she said.

He asked if she was leaving, too. Where she was going.

—North, she said.

She looked down at her boots and kicked each heel against the other, loosening the mud.

—A different kind of winter, she said.

He remained silent. He opened his bag. He took out the food he had brought with him, wrapped in newspapers, and handed it to her.

Then he lifted the child's coat, unfolding it. He held it up for her to see and he took Bia's arm and slipped it into the sleeve. Then the other.

When it was on her he smoothed the collar and checked the buttons. It fit her shoulders though it was a bit short for her; the hem fell above her waist and the cuffs revealed her wrists. Still, Yohan buttoned the coat and Bia blushed, avoiding his eyes.

He did not know what to say. She was examining the buttons on the coat and smiling. They had anchors on them.

—Will you be gone long? he said.

She did not respond. She approached the bicycle. She tilted it away from the tree, gripping its handlebars, waiting for his permission. He nodded.

—Yohan, she said. I'll see you.

She turned and entered the fields that led to the mountains.

He remained under the tree. He watched as she made her way along the country road. A mule approached her and she paused, lifted her palm, and went on, pushing the bicycle and avoiding the puddles.

He thought of Santi in front of the tailor's dummy with his fists raised. His face like a knot. His arms like spears. He thought of the parents the boy could not remember. The boy on the shore and the ships he followed. His quiet violence.

He imagined the tailor as a young man and his journey here, crossing an ocean on a slow-moving ship as he himself did. He wondered whether Kiyoshi had been wearing a uniform. Whether there had been a family and where they were. What the man had fled from, if he had fled at all. What the man had let go of and whether it was possible to regain anything, to search and find it once more. Whether there was someone far from here who remembered him.

He thought of these years as another life within the one he had. As though it were a thing he was able to carry. A small box. A handkerchief. A stone. He did not understand how a life could vanish. How that was even possible. How it could close in an instant before you could reach inside one last time, touch someone's hand one last time. How there would come a day when no one would wonder about the life he had before this one.

She was far away. He could see the shape of her shoulders as she approached the mountains. The child's coat and the spokes of the wheels catching a corner of daylight.

He held his arms. Water continued to fall from the tree.

He was now alone. It had been almost four years since he had first seen her on the deck of a ship. The girl looking for a boat and the kindness of a sailor to show Santi the coast. The gift of an umbrella in the morning rain. The tail of a scarf high in the air, and the boy following as she began to run.

She grew fainter. She kept going.

12

He used to wake early, before the light of morning, and climb the hill beside his home. From there he could see a distant farmhouse with its half-built chimney. This unfinished structure of wood and stones. Six windows like pockets of water.

On some days, if he waited long enough, a candle flame appeared behind one of the windows. This was followed by thc ringing of a bell.

Then the men and the women came out of the woods. They were young. There were children as well, some of them on their own and others on the shoulders or the backs of their fathers and their mothers.

They were members of a theater troupe and they crossed the field, a long line of them wearing old gray shirts and caps and scarves wrapped around their necks.

It was the end of summer. He lay on his stomach, hidden in the grass, and watched as a man appeared at the farmhouse door.

This was his father. He was tall and had tied his hair back with a piece of string. He was the farmhand. And the house was being restored for a landowner whom they never saw, a Japanese man who was a shipbuilder living in Nagasaki.

He gave the troupe buckets and rags, which they slung over their shoulders. Then they surrounded the house.

And under the few stars that remained, against the mountains that were still dark, Yohan watched as the troupe washed the walls and the windows. A few crouched in the grass and some climbed ladders. And still others climbed onto each other to reach the high corners.

He followed the troupe's paths as they circled this structure that resembled to him a shipwrecked vessel. With his father a few of them worked on the chimney with ropes bound to their waists, and the morning was suddenly filled with the echo of hammers as they hung suspended in that low sky, orbiting the rooftop. He watched them part, vanish, then come back together again. Specks of cloth floated in that early light.

This was over fifteen years ago, during the Second World War. Yohan was twelve. And one of the children, high in the air, was Peng, that boy with the gray stripe in his hair, although they would not meet until they were older.

Later, the troupe received food for their work and returned to the woods. They camped there, staying for a week, and then they moved on to the next town, returning again for another season.

They traveled the country. In the towns they performed plays and acrobatics and magic. Sometimes, in the nights, his father would drink at the teahouse and Yohan was allowed to remain outside on the sidewalk, looking through the spaces in the crowd at the performance in the square.

He watched the limbs of marionettes rise and fall. The reflection of a blade. Ribbons of color moving across a stage. A man who opened his coat and all of a sudden a dozen birds emerged from his waist, caught in flight by strings tied to his belt.

He listened to the great tragedies. The love stories.

He clapped when the townspeople clapped.

Then his father found him and they returned home, the sound of the performers fading as they left the town, following the main road, his eyes adjusting from the fires of the lanterns to the dark. He walked as slowly as he could, listening, an energy contained within him that he held until later his father fell asleep and then he returned outside, climbing the hill once more to wait for the troupe to return from the town.

Some nights his father allowed the troupe to practice in the fields; and from the hill Yohan followed their leaping bodies bright from a bonfire. On other nights the children played soccer or took turns riding bicycles. They called down for him. They were quick in the moonlight. Their voices faint.

In the summers, lightning bugs surrounded the land. Hundreds of them blinking in the air as Yohan and the children pedaled through the field or chased a ball. And sometimes even his father would join them, clapping when a goal was scored.

He was surprised by his father's kindness toward them. Around them he revealed a playfulness Yohan would only see a few times in the man's life. He was well into his forties when Yohan was born and he was a solitary man, unused to company, who knew little about children. With a wife who did not survive the birth, he had raised Yohan alone.

Their house was a single room at the edge of the property, closest to the town. They had a mule. A garden.

Yohan knew nothing then of the geography of those years before he left. It wouldn't be until long afterward, a world away, pausing before a map in a store in the hill town, that he would understand how close he had lived to the Sea of Japan and the Russian border.

He had never gone to the ocean. There was a time when he could not imagine farther than a range of mountains. He was unaware that there were ships the size of islands.

It was assumed that he would one day take over his father's work. And when he was old enough he helped care for the land. But for the most part they kept to themselves. Within the boundary of the farm they made their own routes. His father at the barn and Yohan in the hills. His father checking on the farmhouse and Yohan in the garden.

Every evening they ate together and then his father would return outside, to spend a few hours in the shed that stood behind their house. It had been converted into a studio, for his father was an amateur potter, having taken up the hobby when he was young.

On those evenings Yohan could hear the rotations of the kick wheel as he swept the floor of the house or lingered on the road, wondering if the theater troupe had returned from their travels. There were days when, in the fever of the cold, his father worked all night, the smoke of the kiln fire rising past the trees, higher than the smoke of the house's chimney.

And Yohan would find him asleep on the floor, the morning light scaling his clay-covered body. He brought a bucket of water for him and some food, and if it was still early, he took off his father's boots and placed a blanket over him, staying there until the man woke.

On some afternoons he helped his father carry his pots and vases into the town, where he sold them in the market. And for a few hours they sat on a blanket, sometimes bartering for supplies or for food they didn't eat often.

In the market there were craftsmen and peddlers, fishmongers and butchers, Japanese soldiers from the military base, the town doctor with his shoulders stooped from the bag he always carried. These lives that all seemed unknowable and closed as though oceans surrounded each of them.

Most days they returned home with much of what they had brought. But there was also the day when his father had sold everything.

He could only recall it ever happening once: his father helping the old woman who had bought the last two vases, the man's happiness and the lightness of his feet as he walked down the main street. And he remembered his father waving to him from the distance and the boxes, held by strings, rising and falling like miniature houses in his hands.

He was sixteen when his father passed away. One spring morning, not long after the farmhouse was complete, his father was returning home from the hills but never made it, collapsing into the grass. The man was sixty years old.

In the months that followed, Yohan began to care for the farm himself, for an owner he had only met once in his life. He fed the animals. He maintained the renovated farmhouse. He gardened. He went into the town for supplies.

Some nights he stayed, joining the crowd to watch the theater troupe perform in the square.

Afterward, he accompanied them back to the hills, walking beside Peng, whom he knew by then and who was nineteen years old, wanting to ask him about a play they had performed but too shy to.

Instead, Peng's father, with his thick hands, patted him on the back of his neck and spoke to him of the farmhouse and how Yohan's father was missed and then they all fell silent, listening to the rhythm of their slow footsteps on the country road, the troupe's costumes catching a thousand reflections.

That year news arrived that Japan had surrendered. Then came the news that Korea had been divided, a border running along its torso.

The theater troupe never returned. He wondered if they had been traveling in the south, stuck there as so many were.

In the north, where they were, the Russians came.

They took the animals. He watched as the farmhouse, long complete by then, was pulled apart, growing smaller and shorter, its pieces laid across the field. The land had been cheap and he imagined that perhaps the shipbuilder had intended to spend his later years here. That a man who spent his days near water, in ports and harbors, had dreamed of its opposite. He recalled the corridors and the rooms before they vanished, their grandeur and their emptiness. It had been a house for a king.

In its place a factory was built. With the other laborers he was hired to help in its construction. A settlement was created in a field not far from his house. He grew to be friendly with the workers who were from the nearby towns and who would, as the year went on, continue to travel with the military, building.

One night, returning to the house, he went into his father's shed. He stared at the unsold pots and the vases on the shelves, at their shapes and their designs, the illustrations of landscapes. He wondered what would become of them. He reached for one, then hesitated. He thought of them staying here, untouched, through the seasons and the years. He thought of the ones people had purchased, scattered throughout the country. He imagined that somewhere underneath the glaze and the paint there remained his father's hands. That they contained the heat of a kiln and a home that no longer existed. He wondered whether he would be able to recognize them if he saw them again.

He thought of the day they found an abandoned boat on the banks of the nearby river. He was a child then. To Yohan's surprise his father lifted him, climbed into the boat, and began to row.

Halfway to the town he passed the paddle to him and Yohan mimicked his father's movements. He felt tireless. They passed through the forest, past a man casting a net, its web unfurling over the long river. He stared down into the water, the sky in it and the world upside down, the bright trees slipping under him. And his father now lying there, resting his head on Yohan's feet, sighing like some contented animal.

They left the boat in the town and walked home, laughing, this shared secret. Whose boat it was they never discovered. Whether it stayed near that town or whether someone else took it for a journey Yohan did not know.

Standing there, in his father's shed, he knew that there had been, between them, affection and even tenderness. That his father had never been unkind. That in their silences there had been a form of love.

But he had never known him, had never been close to him in the way he witnessed other sons and their fathers.

Perhaps it would have been different if his mother had lived. Perhaps his father had once been someone else and a wife's death had altered him.

Or perhaps his solitude was always there. He would often wonder about that.

But as he grew older he thought less of it, grew accustomed to the days lived. Each day he climbed the hill, as he used to, and helped build the factory. He visited the town. The seasons passed. Then the years. His father a curtained room. His mother, too. This blank space in his life that he was unable to paint.

13

The summer he was nineteen, after his shift, he fell asleep one night at the teahouse. When he woke he found himself on the floor of a room with discolored walls and a single window. A cold bowl of soup lay beside his fingertips.

He fell asleep once more and when it grew dark he opened his eyes to find a girl kneeling beside him. She lifted a spoon to his lips. The taste of broth on his tongue. She smelled of sweat and tea and of something sweet like the smell of a pastry shop.

Her name was Suyon. She was the teahouse hostess. She was twenty-one years old.

She had recognized him.

—The farmhand's boy, she said.

He began to stay with her. During the day he stood in a line at the factory, assembling lightbulbs of various shapes and sizes. Then in the evening he headed into the town and waited for her, peering through a window at the Soviets in their uniforms, playing cards at a corner table.

She was from a family of miners. One of her brothers still worked in the mountains and was gone most seasons.

On her nights off they did not leave the room she rented. He brought her lightbulbs that he stole and she collected them on a table as though they were flowers. She gave him a new shirt. Yohan wrapped a towel around his hands, poured boiling water into a ceramic bowl so that she could wash her hair. Then she washed his.

He liked to lay his head on her lap, look up at her upside down, her hair falling in lines over his face as she covered his ears with her palms.

He luxuriated in the newness of being touched. Of touching someone.

They slept beside each other on the floor. Her body curled into him. Once, when they were unable to sleep, she hung her blanket over the window and they chased each other in that room in the dark, one of them searching while the other hid, the soles of their feet sliding against the old wood floor.

On another night he woke to find her dress hanging above him on a string, the fabric holding the shape of the girl as though she floated there. And as Suyon slept he reached up to touch it, feeling the thinness and the age of the silk, feeling the years contained there, wondering if those years were the girl's or someone else's.

Lying there, on those nights, she would speak to him. She told him about her youth. Her parents. Her brothers. She wiggled her toes in the moonlight and he did not know why but he copied her.

—They're older, she said. Two of them. They used to carry me on their shoulders. They stole horses and I rode with them. They spied on the girls bathing in the river. Dared each other to descend the banks and touch their clothes. In the field we took turns cutting Father's hair, and each other's. Father worked in the mines first, then my brothers. I would head to the mountains and wait for them. In the evening we walked the road home, leading the oldest, who by then was unable to see in the dark. Night blindness. He was not yet thirty years old when there was an accident underground. He is the one I think of the most. I am sitting on his shoulders and gripping his wrists. The light sound of his boots. The ash smell of his hair. This girl's wish to touch the stars granted by a brother who couldn't see them.

The surviving brother came home one morning. Yohan was pulled outside. He was pushed against the wall and the man struck him and struck him again.

Yohan fought back. He formed his hands into fists. He tucked in his shoulders and sought the impact of a body. He hit him as hard as he could. He struck the brother's face and his chest and he fought.

But the brother was stronger. Yohan was dragged down the street, away from the town. He thought he heard clapping. A dog followed them. The taste of his blood already mixing with what remained of the taste of her.

He was left outside of the town. He crawled toward the shade of a tree. With the eye he could open he looked down at his hands. The sleeves of his new shirt. He had lost a shoe. His hair was covered in dirt and a drop of the man's spit remained on his chin. He waited there to see if anyone would appear, whether Suyon would come looking for him.

He looked around him. The light was fading. A group

of factory workers were on their way to the hills. The dog roamed the grass. In the town a man was climbing a ladder, lighting the streetlamps.

Yohan leaned against the tree; the earth under him cooled. He stared at the flatness of the country and then the mountains. The factory workers were far along the road, their bodies growing smaller.

A military truck appeared. It was blaring a song on the radio and as it passed the men they began to dance. They stood in the middle of the road, in the last light, and they did not stop, even after the truck was gone and the song faded. They twisted their hips. They kicked the dust. His body numb, his face half-closed, Yohan was unaware of his foot tapping the ground.

He never saw her again. That fall he left with a group of workers. He was given wages, food, and housing. He traveled from town to city, working in rubber and munitions factories.

In 1949, when he was twenty, along with all of them, he was conscripted.

A year after that, when the war started, he crossed the border into the south, following a great mass of them with their new boots and their weapons, their bodies like a thousand trees as the landscape, in a single step, changed forever.

In that ruined country he would move across that new architecture of rubble and debris and broken rooftops, lift a fallen door with his rifle, find a boy asleep on a mat.

He stopped, startled. It was as though he had discovered a palace. The child deep in dreams, surrounded by cups and pottery and fabrics and mirrors, dozens of them reflecting the sky and him.

He turned to see if the other men had noticed. He lowered the door, careful not to wake the boy, and left.

In those first months he thought often of the theater troupe, wondering where they had gone. He found a pair of marionettes hanging high up in the trees, their legs swinging as he walked under them. He passed the bombed remains of a theater where a dog lay beside a tin cup full of rainwater and a pile of costumes it had made for a bed.

Crossing a river, he caught two girls underwater, looking up at him, wide-eyed, their mouths as small as coins, as though they had willed themselves to be invisible. On the banks he left them what he could. A spare shoelace. Food and a pocketknife.

That year of ceaseless movement, continuing south. He traveled mostly on foot. Their helmets casting strange shadows. They searched abandoned homes, relishing the momentary freedom of resting in a room and looking out as though it were their own house. They navigated unrecognizable structures, collecting men who had been left behind.

His senses grew accustomed to the sudden lightning of ammunition. The gray dust that was everywhere. All the open windows and doors and the weather taking shape on the floors.

He saw a river catch on fire, stunned at how such a thing was possible. He found a foot sprouting from the earth, its toes splayed. Then the toes wilted. He was unsure if he had seen the movement. A trick of the mind, perhaps. A trick of shadow. They were moving quickly and he lost sight of it. A useless thought overwhelmed him: the nakedness of the foot and whether someone had taken the shoes.

On a cargo train one night he sat surrounded by other soldiers. The cold air filled with their coughing, the glow of cigarettes, and their breaths as they leaned against each other for warmth. There were wounded men in the car behind them and on occasion they could hear a muffled scream over the engine noises as a medic attempted to operate while they traveled.

It was winter. The cars were missing their doors and he watched the dim stain of an airplane flying above the valley. The stars were endless. He listened to the wind and the sleeping men. He smelled the persistent smell of burning and stale blood that he was already used to. He felt his body grow heavy, lulled by the rhythm of the train.

He slipped in and out of dreams. Snow was falling.

Up ahead, in a long field, shapes appeared, caught in the moonlight. It was a family, perhaps, a man and a woman and their children, all of them standing in the snow above the wreckage of a town.

The man dipped into a collapsed rooftop as though he were swimming. His wife gathered her skirt against her thighs as she climbed a hill of rubble and white, the up-turned bowl over her head swaying with her steps. Two boys appeared from the depths of a crater, their hands rising to grab the rim.

Pockets were filled. With what, Yohan was too far to see. They worked in silence, taking what they could. Their arms dipped into the wreckage, their hands aglow, crystallized, as if what they held were only snow.

For the first time in what seemed like years, Yohan thought of his father. Thought of the man with his hat the color of bark. How, during the first snow of the season, Yohan once saw him jump in the field in the evening, believing he was alone, some private joy as he clicked his ankles in the air, that hat shining like a star on his head.

He thought of how whatever fire his father had within him he had kept.

And he understood that he would never be able to hold all the years that had gone in their entirety. That those years would begin to loosen, break apart, slip away. That there would come a time when there was just a corner, a window, a smell, a gesture, a voice to gather and assemble.

The train continued through the valley. A soldier moved closer to him. He also had been staring out into the field at the family. His fingernails were covered in dried mud. There was vomit on his shirt and he leaned against his rifle in exhaustion.

They had not yet recognized each other. This young man who used to walk a country road with him in the evening, who once climbed houses, somersaulted, and voiced marionettes.

In a year they would be standing in an orange grove

with a patrol unit, frozen, watching a single goat on a ridge as a whistling filled the air and the land exploded, burying them.

On the train he lifted the blanket off his shoulder and offered Yohan half of it. Then he nodded toward the field, his eyes unblinking.

—Snow hunters, Peng said, and together they watched the scavenging family for as long as they could, the way they moved across the snow like acrobats, their bright forms growing smaller in the night as the train sped.

14

He often returned to the tree above the hill town. He went there in the mornings when it was still dark. He carried an empty shoulder bag and pushed his bicycle up the slope.

Through the years Yohan had begun to deliver newspapers. He followed his assigned route, reached into his bag, threw a paper against a door. He raced through the streets. When his path crossed with the others he clicked his flashlight and they signaled back.

They vanished as fast as they appeared. That hour filled with the sound of wheels on the cobblestone and the blinking lights of the bicyclists spread out over the town and the coast until they faded, one by one.

On those mornings he was tired and yet awake. His body sluggish and yet alert. The heat had already started. He hung his damp shirt on a branch and lay down on the ridge, pulling his hat over his eyes, feeling the grass against him.

He waited for daylight, the familiar shapes of the town to distinguish themselves, the gray and the blue of the water. On a far beach where a hotel had been built, umbrellas stood closed and scattered along the sand.

He turned. He tipped his hat back and looked inland. He lay there resting his chin against his hands, facing the distance where there were now fences alongside the road. There were also two farmhouses at the base of the mountains. Smoke began to rise out of their chimneys.

Then the horses appeared. Bays and roans crossing the grass and grazing in the paddocks. He counted them, as he had begun to do.

Some mornings one or two of them jumped the fence and wandered the road until a farmhand or a truck driver noticed. Once, they climbed the hill and gathered on the ridge where Yohan was, gazing out across the rooftops and the sea. And the town woke to them, their long shadows on the slope.

And still there were days when the farm children appeared, sleepy-eyed, looking for the hand who gave them rope to repair. He watched the man tie one end to the children's boots and they sat in the field with their legs extended, undoing the braids and rebraiding them. Their fingers moving like birds.

It was full daylight now. The mountains were visible, the road empty.

He stood. He reached for his shirt. He slung his bag over his shoulder and pushed the bicycle down the meadow, heading into the town.

At the gates of the church he waved toward the cottage where he knew Peixe was writing. He passed the stores, smelling coffee and the ovens of the bakery. He could hear voices from a high window. Between two buildings there was the glimpse of the coast where a group of dugout canoes were spread out across the water.

At the tailor's shop he unlocked the door, the bell chiming, and pushed the bicycle across the room, storing it in the room where Kiyoshi once slept. He boiled water for coffee and ate a piece of bread with butter. He showered and changed into a suit, tying the tie in front of a mirror he had hung behind his bedroom door.

He returned to the shop, lifting the shutters. The room filled with daylight. He flipped the sign on the window. He picked lint off the shoulders of the tailor's dummy. At his desk he looked at his schedule book. He lifted a suit from a rack and placed it on his worktable. He turned the ceiling fan on and sat down.

It was the first months of 1963. He was thirty-four years old. In the town the day began and Yohan worked, undoing the seams of the fabric.

Little in the world of the tailor's shop had changed. All the tools and the machines, the threads and the scissors and the needles, remained the way Kiyoshi had organized them. Fabrics were stored on the shelves and in the drawers by material and color. The worktables stood in the same places, though the one on the left wall had gone untouched. The red curtain hung at the back of the shop, swaying when he propped the shop door open on the warmest days. He boiled water with the same kettle, drank from the same cups. On the second floor the room across from his was still used for storage, the wooden crates filled with spare supplies.

There were new customers now, new storeowners and new wives and husbands and new styles for dresses and suits, but there were also the people who had come to the shop for over a decade. He delivered clothes to the woman with the pet bird, listening as she had conversations with her dead husband. Children whose church outfits he used to tailor were older now but they came, as did a government man who had retired five years before.

There were the farmers, too, appearing with their shirts tucked into a clean pair of pants and their boots polished and their hair combed for a night in the town, bringing their young sons and daughters who pressed their faces against the windows of the pastry shop. They waited in the kitchen with their mother, drinking soda while the father, in his politeness, remained outdoors.

When he was finished Yohan crossed the street and bought the children cups of avocado cream and a bag of coconut cookies. The father wiped his palm against his shirt and shook Yohan's hand and then the family continued into the town, browsing the storefront windows.

In these years he had become fluent in Portuguese.

He now understood how the words were shaped and pronounced, it was no longer an effort, and he conversed with the townspeople, asking them about their days and their families and commenting on the weather. He joked with his customers. He visited the barbershop and traded gossip.

He spent more time exploring the neighborhoods beyond his own, handing out advertisements he had written for the shop.

With a package of clothes under his arm he was often seen throughout the entire town and the harbor. He was recognized and greeted, though no one ever used his name.

—It is the tailor, they all said, as though he had been here always.

His friend, the sailor, had passed away two years before. The ship had docked one day and the sailor was not there. The others, younger, shook their heads.

—I'm sorry, they said, giving him papers to sign and unloading his fabrics.

And Yohan was unable to control the shaking of his body as he hauled his supplies up the street, refusing to rest and wipe his face and ignoring the people who had stopped on the sidewalk, confused, until someone rushed over to help.

He no longer ordered supplies from Japan. He now worked with a textile mill north of the town.

But he still wore the clothes Kiyoshi had made for him, mending them when a collar was frayed or a button came loose.

That old tailor whom he often missed. There were days when he paused in his work and listened, waiting for a noise, the sound of movement behind him: the quiet hum of another sewing machine, a chair adjusting, the patter of slippers or the flare of matches.

He heard nothing but his own machine and the street and yet he stayed still, waiting.

One time the scent of the old man appeared in the air: some combination of tobacco and citrus and soap. It was fleeting yet he was certain he had smelled it, but he did not know where it had come from, whether it had been someone at the window or from the shop itself, as though a part of the man remained in the tables, in the air of the boxes, in the fabrics themselves.

He looked toward the door and recalled the day he had entered the shop for the first time: the ping of a bell, Kiyoshi's slow movements.

It was true that they had never spoken much to each other. So it surprised him that there were times when all he remembered was Kiyoshi's voice. It reminded Yohan of fall in the country where he was born and where he had spent his first twenty years, the dry wind and all the leaves falling from the mountains into the town. Kiyoshi, whose voice, when he spoke, sounded like leaves spinning in the air.

There were days when he believed there was nothing more to come. That there was nothing else. He had arrived and he had stayed. He had made a life. He had entered the future.

And in these hours, in this silence, the shop seemed larger to him, as though each night as he slept the floors extended, the walls grew; they carried with them the lives they once had as trees, some quiet tremor he could not detect.

He thought: he lived in a forest. He would wake one day to see branches in the spaces. The shadows of foliage, ivy. The tailor's dummy standing in the corner, rooted into the earth.

He continued to sleep in the room above the shop. The woman he had seen on his first night here, on the balcony across the street, had married. Sometimes it happened that they looked outside from their windows at the same time and they waved to each other.

They had once attempted to share a clothesline to hang their laundry but someone stole their shirts, though how they did so, at this height, Yohan still did not know. It had been a fanciful experiment but they had shared that rope, briefly, and sometimes he liked to imagine it still there.

Now across that space they had conversations, asking each other about their days, about when it would rain. And once she asked in a loud voice, for the town to hear, how she could make her ugly husband more like Yohan. Then the husband appeared by the window and lifted her and she screamed in delight as he took her into a curtained room.

In this room there was still the desk and the chair. A single lightbulb and the mattress on the floor. The cookie tin and the teacup he had found long ago.

On some nights when the shop was closed he entered the tailor's room. It took him a year to return here. Whatever Kiyoshi had left remained. His slippers lay under the cot. His shirts were hanging in a narrow closet. There was the single nail on the wall. The chest full of clothes.

On the nightstand there was a stack of books. Sometimes he flipped through them. They were adventure stories. They were written in Japanese but he had begun to forget some words so he could not read all of them.

He lay on the cot with a book on his chest. He looked up at the wall where he had hung the photograph of Kiyoshi in front of the plantation house during the Second World War. Peixe had given it to him.

He wondered, as he often did, what life the tailor had led before this one. He thought of Kiyoshi as a young man and saw the youth of his face and saw a family and then saw him in uniform, his hands stitching a wound on the stomach of a boy in the Russian Far East.

On those nights he thought of the sailor, too. Of his wife and children. He wondered if they still lived in a coastal village in Japan and whether the wife still worked at a hotel.

He had written a letter to her once, not long after the sailor passed away. He never sent it. It lay now in the tin cookie box in his room, on top of the business card and the letter of employment he had carried with him nine years ago.

In Kiyoshi's room he placed the book back on the nightstand. Then he stood and made the bed, flattening the blanket, erasing the shape of his body.

15

Peixe was forty-one years old now. They had begun to see more of each other. A pair of reading glasses stayed around his neck at all times, tied with Yohan's packaging twine. His hair was graying and he liked to joke about it.

He said, —*Alfaiate,* you're looking at your future self, and he laughed as they walked the rows of his garden, watering the plants and the vegetables, tossing fertilizer onto the soil.

For his birthday one year Yohan bought him a new cane. Its handle had been carved in the shape of a boat. Pleased, Peixe twirled it and even attempted a dance in the garden. Then he pretended it was a sword and lunged at Yohan, who ducked and picked up a branch, and, like children, they dueled until they heard the priest shouting and they looked down at the trampled tomatoes.

As he aged, Peixe had become more youthful. One night Yohan was woken by a loud noise at his window. He saw Peixe standing in the street, leaning on his cane and throwing rocks at him.

Peixe was dressed in a suit. He had never seen him in a suit before. It was the color of the beach and the fashion was many years old. A flower was tucked into his lapel.

He called to Yohan to dress himself.

—And bring me a tie, he said, and Yohan did, appearing outside a few minutes later, tying it for him under a streetlamp.

Peixe slid his arm around Yohan's and led him down the hill.

He was taken to a nightclub. The hostess seemed to know Peixe, showing them to a table that had been reserved. They ordered cocktails and faced a small stage where a jazz band performed with a singer who wore a slim blue dress and swayed her hips.

They stayed all night. A woman approached them and Peixe took her in his arms and settled her on his lap. Another woman appeared and took Yohan's wrist and before he understood what was happening he was on the dance floor, the woman with her arms around him and smelling of perfume and her lips painted. She moved into him and he felt her hips against his as he held her waist and they circled the dimly lit floor.

He searched the woman's eyes, trying to remember if they had met before.

She said, —You can't dance, and he said, —No, and smiled, and she tilted her head back and laughed and her neck shone in the nightclub lights.

She told him to follow and took the lead.

They spent the evening and the early morning together, the girl teaching him how to dance, his jacket collecting a strand of her hair.

Her name was Ana. She had moved here from Brasília a few months before. Her mother was Spanish and her father Portuguese. She was twenty-seven years old and was a schoolteacher. It was the first time she had been to the nightclub as well. It was also the first time she had worn lipstick.

For a month there was a romance. She would wait until it was late in the night, when Yohan's neighbors were already sleeping, and slip into the shop. He would take her upstairs and they would spend what remained of the night in that room with its low ceiling, Ana tilting her head as she went to him.

She drank coffee and liked to brush her hair. She wrapped spare fabrics over her body and he sometimes carried her up and down the house, visiting the rooms.

He made her a dress. He measured her body. He fell asleep with his ear against her belly button, listening to her breathing, feeling the energy of her. This chamber inside her skin.

They told no one of each other. And there were moments when he thought the months would go on like this. But they didn't. He was never sure why. Just that whatever had contained them faded. They both understood this without saying so. It had been short-lived, a flare.

He used to see her on occasion in the market or on the street. They would wave and ask how the other was getting along. They would wish each other well and move on, she walking in one direction, he in another. And he would think fondly of those days with her.

Then came a day when they passed each other without stopping. Perhaps it had been unintentional. Perhaps they had been busy or had grown shy of each other. But the moment, as he shut his eyes and fell asleep, receded so that by morning he wasn't sure whether it had ever happened.

One day, helping Peixe mop the floors of the church, he saw the advertisement for a job delivering newspapers. Waiting at the office, Yohan looked behind him at the boys and the girls waiting as well. They stuffed their hands in their pockets and made faces at him when the hiring man wasn't looking.

He was given a shorter route than the children. He bought a bicycle. Every morning before dawn he delivered the newspapers. Some mornings when he was finished he climbed the hill and watched the horses. Other times he bicycled along the coastal road, stopping beside the land where the settlement once was and where the plantation house had been renovated and turned into a school, the field used for soccer tournaments that he and Peixe went to on the weekends.

They sat high in the bleachers, Peixe insisting, and they looked out over the field and followed the bright glow of uniforms.

Most of the people who had once lived in the settlement were gone. He knew that some of the fishermen had formed a village near a small bay but that was all. He did not know where the rest had gone, did not know whether they had stayed as a group or had scattered, moving across this country or even farther, across oceans.

He thought of the blind juggler who tossed hats and shoes. He thought of a boy with an imaginary spyglass, facing the coast. A girl's lips brushing his ear as she spoke. The touch of a hand against his own.

He hoped that wherever they all were, their lives were how they wished it to be.

A goal was scored. Peixe stood, lifting his cane and shouting, and Yohan joined him.

In this way the days passed. Those days became years. Those years a life. In the evenings he climbed the old stairs into his room. Standing by the window, he pressed a cold washcloth against his neck. A fan spun. He listened to music coming from the nightclub. An airplane. The voice of the woman across the street.

16

One summer the bell above the shop door rung once and stopped. He had just opened the shop and it was empty. From his worktable he looked up.

He saw a girl with a hand in the air, her fingers closing over the bell, muting the sound. She had a small nose and a pointed chin and her hair was pale and cut short like a boy's.

She was wearing a pair of sandals and a green dress that ended at her shins. The shoulder straps were thin but sturdy and there were buttons on the ends. He appreciated the simplicity of the design and the simplicity of her form there by the door, this shadowed pose, that arc of her arm and her on her tiptoes.

He waited for her to say something, to explain herself, but she didn't. She stood transfixed by the bell. Then she released it and pushed it with her fingertips, causing the ringing once more. Not once did her eyes leave the bell, as if she were waiting for it to fall. She brought both of her hands toward her ears.

—Is it a bother? he finally said.

He spoke in Portuguese.

She shook her head. She pointed out the window. She said the other day she could hear it from the street. She said they sounded new. She liked the way the sound touched her skin.

—Like this, she said, and shook her hands beside her head and made a buzzing noise with her lips.

—Yes, he said, and laughed and she laughed, too.

She had not moved from the door. The light was clear and strong outside and she was still a silhouette. Then she turned toward him and approached and they looked at each other for a moment.

He lowered his head. When he glanced at her she was looking around at the boxes and the tables and the fabrics against the walls and the shirts wrapped in paper. He noticed a bracelet on her wrist; it was made of colored threads, old, simple, and elegant.

She approached the tailor's dummy and examined the stitches on its stomach. She looked beyond him toward the curtain. There was a familiarity to her that he could not place.

—You've been here long? she said.

She meant the shop. Her voice was quiet, deliberate. She stood beside the tailor's dummy, facing the window with her hands behind her back. The air was still. Pedestrians walked by and their shadows cut through the shop.

Her short hair was wet. It was the color of the morning and she smelled of the ocean.

He shrugged, even though she could not see him. He did not know if nine years was a long time or not.

She smiled, sliding her fingernails along her forearms.

—It's nice, she said, and he looked away again at the things she saw and the quiet and the light and he could not help but agree, it was nice at this hour and the many other hours and days; and he felt the pride of that, those words and this shop, and knew that he was blushing although he did not think she noticed, she was now looking up at the ceiling, at the small spider in the air.

Beside the tailor's dummy stood an umbrella, closed

and leaning against the corner of the room. She picked it up and twirled it once in her hands.

She smiled again.

She said, —I'll take it back now, and he looked at her, perplexed, and then he felt a weight on his tongue; then his heart.

He sat there, stunned. He was unable to speak, unable to rise from his chair.

She laughed.

—Okay, she said. You keep it for a while longer.

She returned the umbrella to its corner and looked at him once more. She was still smiling. She shifted her weight from one foot to the other, studying him, waiting.

—Yohan, she said, and in that moment he heard the remnant of a child's voice that used to call his name.

Before he could respond she abruptly turned and opened the door, the bell ringing as she returned to the sidewalk.

He rushed outside. He was flooded by the heat and the daylight. He squinted, lifting a hand. But what had driven him slipped away and he stopped. A doubt had entered him. And he grew afraid, although what he was afraid of he was unsure.

He remained by the shop window. A neighbor greeted

him. He spotted the green of her dress against the pale of the buildings and watched as she moved in and out of the crowd and the sunlight. He followed the curve of her bare shoulders. The beat of her sandals on the cobblestone. Then she was gone.

He began to look for her but did not know where to begin, searching the town for someone he had not seen in five years. In some ways he did not know whom to look for, his mind returning to the girl she was. He visited Peixe in case he had seen her but the groundskeeper mentioned nothing and Yohan said nothing either, keeping her arrival within him.

It seemed possible that he had been wrong, that there had been some kind of misunderstanding in the words she had said in the shop, that it was not her voice he had heard, that it was someone else.

Then a few days later the bell rung, the door opened, and she stood in the same place as she did the first time. She kept silent and from his worktable he watched her.

—Okay, she said, worrying her fingers as if she wanted to say something else or was waiting for him to say something.

She looked around at the shop as she did before and hurried out the door.

She did not visit again until the next day. This time she stayed. She was wearing her green dress and her sandals and she remained standing at a distance from him. She had combed her short hair. She fiddled with her bracelet and he wondered if she had woven it or had purchased it or whether someone had given it to her. Her movements in the shop were awkward, as though she was no longer used to small spaces. He brought her tea.

That first week Bia never stayed long, her visits still unexpected. He never knew what to say when she came. He waited for her to tell him where she was staying but she didn't. He waited for her to tell him what her life had been like these past five years.

When he asked where she had been she replied, —All over, and said nothing else.

It had always been like this. The hour passed in the only way they knew how. But now, in their reticence and their shyness, they were remembering each other. As if they were each a lens to hold and peer into.

In this way an ease began to form around them.

—I'll see you soon, she always said, whenever they parted.

He was never sure if he would see her the following the day or the week after or whether this was the last time.

But she continued to come. Sometimes she visited in the mornings. Other times in the afternoons and there were also times when she waited outside until he noticed her in the window, leaning against Kiyoshi's bicycle, which she had kept all these years.

She was twenty-four now. And every day she sat where Kiyoshi once did, curled on the chair and drinking tea. If he had clothes to tailor, she let him work and watched the passing pedestrians.

And although there were days when she seemed to be how he remembered her, she had become more confident and assured, he heard it when she spoke, that change in her voice now that she was older. When customers entered she greeted them, complimenting the women on the dresses they wore or the men on their suits, and they looked at her with curiosity, wondering who she was.

They only ever saw each other in the shop. She shut her eyes against the sunlight, tilting her head to one side as she often did, a gesture he would grow accustomed to and then expect, and then love her for it, her body moving as though some part of her he had not yet seen was suddenly revealed.

But there were also times when he was unable to move, unable to look at her, afraid he had been imagining this and that she wouldn't be there. It seemed possible. And when he considered this an emptiness overwhelmed him, as if he were no longer here, that there was just this shell of a body bent over a table. And even as he continued to hear her behind him he felt a sadness, though for what he could not say. It seemed to have nothing to do with her at all but rather a fragment of some old thought.

But she was there of course, she had not left. She stood by the far wall, holding her elbows and browsing the shelves as though she had entered a library.

Once, as he was hemming a pair of trousers, he heard her rummaging in the closet. Then it was silent and when he looked toward the back of the shop she was gone.

She emerged from the kitchen a few minutes later, through the curtain, wearing a suit. It was gray, one Kiyoshi had made for him. She wore a hat with a short brim and it fell past her eyes. A dark blue necktie hung around her neck.

—Help, she said.

The jacket was large for her, its shoulders too wide, but he spun her around, admiring her. Holding her, he walked her toward the window and she stood there looking out, the hat tilted on her head. The passersby paused, waiting to see if she would move.

She didn't. She stayed there frozen in a pose. Later, she changed into a dress Yohan had made and returned to the window. The neighborhood children gathered on the street and waved their arms to distract her. Every so often she winked at them or leaned forward and shouted, —Boo! and they scattered in mock terror.

She began to assist him. She came early, bringing fruit and cookies, and rushed across the room to make coffee, her bare feet light over the floor. She accompanied him on his deliveries, waiting on the sidewalk as he entered a building.

At the shop she wrapped the tailored clothes and dusted the shelves, following the perimeter of the room. She stood by Yohan's side with a notebook while he measured a man for a suit.

When the shop was closed they spent hours listening to the radio, tuning in to a station that played French songs, Bia tapping her feet and mumbling along, practicing the language. Or they listened to the news, the mur-

mur of a man's voice filling the room as he spoke of the cities, other countries.

Each day for an hour in the afternoon she sat in front of Kiyoshi's sewing machine and Yohan would peer over her shoulder as she chewed on her tongue and practiced stitches on the spare pieces of fabric he had given her.

He wondered what Kiyoshi would have thought of her there at his worktable. It had never occurred to him until recently that he had been the tailor's first and only apprentice. And to this day he did not know why the man had taken him, did not know whether Kiyoshi had volunteered or whether he had accepted a proposal that had been offered.

In that first year he woke one night to Kiyoshi shaking him, unaware that in his sleep he had been screaming. He was unable to focus; his eyes had lost clarity. His clothes were wet. Kiyoshi took him into his arms and lifted him. He drew water for a bath and brought the shop's footstool and sat beside the tub, pouring the warm water over Yohan and scrubbing his back. He had sat in the water hugging his knees, unwilling to let go of Kiyoshi's hand.

He wondered if his life now would seem as far away as so many of the years did. It seemed impossible to him, watching her hunched over the table in her green dress, sewing.

One day she brought him a roll of fabric, carrying it on her shoulder. Yohan held the door open as she pushed through the entrance, her body damp with sweat.

—They were just throwing it away, she said. At the textile factory. It is new, no? The building. There's more if you want. I could only carry one. Good stuff, no?

She wiped her face with her forearms. She slapped the fabric and dust burst over her and she shrieked and Yohan, laughing, ran into the kitchen, soaking a hand towel under the faucet.

When he returned she was sitting down. Standing above her, he wiped the dust from her skin. He started with her face and then moved the towel over her shoulders and her hands.

They did not speak. He felt her watching him. Her fingers were calloused. Dirt was buried under her fingernails. He flattened her palms. With his index finger he followed the lines on her skin. She tilted her head and let him.

Later that day he shut his eyes, enjoying the sun in the room. A shadow passed. He heard movement but kept his eyes closed. Slowly, she slipped her hand through his hair. She traced the outline of his crooked nose and the scar. She placed her lips against his eyelid. Then, releasing him, she moved to his other eye. The gesture was light, almost hesitant. He felt her breath on his forehead.

How completely time could abandon someone. How far it could leap. He heard the bell chime and opened his eyes.

17

In the late evening she circled the street on her bicycle, a carousel moving in and out of the streetlights.

—Yohan! she called, and he leaned out of his room, raised a finger to his lips, and hurried through the shop.

She followed him past the curtain in the doorway and up the stairs. She had never been up here before. She paused by his room, her eyes exploring the space, and then she continued to follow the stairs, heading up to the rooftop.

The night was clear and warm. He turned the chairs over and they sat beside each other, resting their feet on the rooftop's edge. Somewhere a trumpet was playing.

The world had softened, its edges vanishing. They found the few windows that were still lit. They pointed at one and then another, and they imagined lives. He imagined everyone that had been a part of his own behind each square, that they had always been there, in rooms not far from him.

He heard Bia say, —Oh.

Then the sound of something hitting the street. She lifted her feet and he saw that she was missing a sandal.

They peered down over the roof. Her sandal lay on the sidewalk, caught in the glare of a streetlamp. They waited to see if anyone came but no one did. The street remained empty. They kept watching the sandal as though it would come to life.

Her hands and her wrists hovered over the edge of the roof and he tried to recall whether that part of her had changed. He thought of the child that she was and tried to find her in the woman he saw now. He thought of her carrying Santi and the two of them sitting all day with patience at the market, selling their bracelets.

And he thought of how it came to be that he was here on this rooftop in this town, in this country, with Bia, who had resurfaced into his life. He wondered if she had come here before and they had missed each other. And again he wondered what these past years had been like for her, what she had seen and what she had left, what she was expecting to find here by coming back, if she was expecting anything at all.

They continued to lean against the rooftop's edge. The air had cooled. Moonlight had settled on the rooftops of the town.

—One morning I woke up, she said, and I remembered you. Just like that. Maybe you were in my dream.

Her voice had slowed. She was staring at the few remaining window lights with her head resting on her hands. In the sky a small shadow flew over a television antenna.

—Just like that, she said. All these years later. I remembered you standing there in the rain on the dock with a bag over your shoulder. And I remembered you looked very tired and sad with your old man's suit and crooked nose and your short hair. And I remembered giving the sailor my blue umbrella to give to you and you holding it, unsure of how to use it. And then you waved to the sailors who were unloading their cargo and you placed a hand to your chest as though you were praying or sighing or frightened. And I saw the days here. I saw Santi and Kiyoshi. And I saw you on that hill, waiting for me with a bicycle and a child's coat. I thought of the war that you survived but that stayed in your voice and your steps. And I thought of those years that I had carried but had not seen in a long time.

—So I stood. I ate a piece of bread and drank a glass of water. I combed my hair and dressed. Then I got on the bicycle and rode, wondering where you, Yohan, had gone.

Bia fell asleep on the rooftop that night. She slept on the chair, leaning against the edge of the roof. For a while he stayed with her and then he slipped his hands under her arms and lifted her.

He crossed the rooftop. He carried her down the steps into the kitchen. He opened the door to the room there and laid her on the cot. He pulled a blanket over her but changed his mind. She was warm. He unclasped her sandal and placed it on the floor. She lay on her side, asleep, and he moved his hand over her hair, once, still unused to its short length.

He hurried into the shop, passing her bicycle, and went outside to retrieve her other sandal.

It was late, the street quiet. He stood there on the

sidewalk and faced the tailor's shop. In the window glass he could see the building behind him, its open balcony doors. Above that the moon.

He looked down and saw himself. His reflection vague and his hand holding a sandal. He and his father used to cut each other's hair. They used to scatter the clumps and the strands throughout the woods for the birds to use as nests.

He thought of how long ago that was. How he used to believe nests became trees.

18

He woke the next day to find Kiyoshi's room empty. The bed had been made, the sheets tucked, and the blanket folded. He leaned against the doorway. A fly circled the corner of the ceiling. He looked around at the nightstand, the photograph, the chest of clothes, and the slippers under the bed. He looked down at the mattress one more time to see if her shape was still visible.

It was as though no one had stayed here at all. In the emptiness of the room he knew that she was gone again.

He left the shop, leaving the sign on the door how it was. It was a clear day. The stores were opening. Inside the bakery a line had already formed. Above him, through the open balcony door, his neighbor watered plants while her husband turned the dial of a television.

He climbed the hill. He passed the church and entered the meadow, heading toward the ridge. He waited under the tree, scanning the coast and the farmlands where the horses were already grazing. The road was empty. He raised his hands above his eyes and kept waiting.

He did not hear the footsteps until they were near him. He turned to see Peixe breathing heavily from the climb. The man, dressed in a torn shirt, took his glasses off and wiped his brow with a handkerchief.

—There's still some life in it, Peixe said, tapping his leg with his cane.

He took Peixe's arm to help him sit but the groundskeeper shook his head. From his pocket he took out a spyglass.

—My mother's, he said. She found it on the shore. Many years ago. A star in the sand, she called it. She picked it up and looked into it. She swiveled her body. In that circle she saw the silhouette of a man rowing toward her. A fisherman. She married him three months later.

—I used to stand here and use it to watch the camp, watch Kiyoshi tossing rocks into the air. Or look for my father. They fished along the coast. In the shallow water.

Shellfish. Sometimes I carry it with me all day. I don't know why. Here. Try.

Yohan extended the spyglass and looked through the lens. He spotted seabirds on a tall boulder. The flag of the new hotel. The bright red of a T-shirt hanging on a rooftop clothesline.

Peixe tilted his head back and studied the tree.

—I have never climbed this tree, he said.

He rubbed his leg. He grinned. He took Yohan's shoulder.

He said, —Help, and dropped his cane and leaned his weight against him.

Yohan, laughing, wrapped his arms around the man's waist and lifted him as high as he could. Peixe reached for a branch. Yohan formed a step with his hands and soon the groundskeeper sat high in the tree.

Yohan picked up the cane and hooked it over a branch. He returned the spyglass and Peixe leaned back, shutting his eyes.

—Yohan, he said. Thank you. I'll stay here for a while.

He didn't know how Peixe would climb down. With his eyes still closed, Peixe tapped his arms.

—There's still life in these, he said, and he waved and Yohan waved back.

He was halfway across the meadow when he heard again Peixe's voice.

—Try the fishing village, he said.

A wind was blowing. In the distance, high up in the tree, he saw his friend raise the spyglass out toward the water.

He walked past the harbor and the ships, following the coastal road south. When he was away from the town he left the road and climbed down onto a beach. He continued along the sand, moving with the curve of the shore.

At the base of a high cliff there was a small bay and a cluster of homes beyond a grove. They were shanties and lean-tos with rooftops made of tin, thatch, and some scavenged tiles. Smoke rose from their thin flues.

Men and women appeared. They crossed through the grove and approached the dugout canoes on the beach. They passed him and some nodded as they leaned forward and gripped the canoes and pushed, the hulls cutting the sand.

Near the grove an open satchel was leaning against a log. He kneeled. A winter coat had been folded into it and he saw the worn collar and a frayed sleeve. The color of the fabric had faded. He touched the coat and held the buttons with the anchors on them and he began to cry.

The villagers let him be. He wiped his face. He loosened his necktie and sat on the log beside the satchel.

Yohan spent the day there. He watched families head out into the sea while others returned. He listened to the swing of hinges, footsteps, and seabirds.

A man approached him, carrying a bundle of newspaper under his arm. He was tall and had long, pale hair. His hands were dark from ash. He rubbed his eyes, yawned, and offered the package to him. Inside there were six fish he had caught. Yohan shook his head, thanking him, and the man shrugged, placing the bundle into a basket.

In the afternoon, voices of children broke through the trees and they gathered around him, asking if he was the tailor and what he was doing here. They took turns examining his necktie and his jacket lying beside him.

A girl was carrying a soccer ball. Yohan took off his shoes and played soccer with the children on the beach. He ran. They chased him. They left a thousand footprints in the sand.

He helped a family build a fire. He returned to the log and shared his cigarettes with the villagers. A man, hesitating, brought him a shirt and a piece of string and

Yohan mended the tear. Then the man brought the clothes of his children and he mended those, too.

Toward the evening he saw a group of small dugout canoes approaching the bay. They came from the south, following the coast, scattered along the water.

Bia was among them. She was wearing a long-brimmed hat made of straw and had tied the skirt of her green dress around her legs. She paddled into the bay.

Around her, fishermen jumped into the water and pulled their canoes to shore. They carried their nets and their buckets of shellfish and climbed the beach toward their homes.

He approached her. He thought she would disembark as well but she stayed, sitting there in the boat as it rocked from the tide. The brim of her hat shaded her eyes so that he couldn't tell where she was looking.

In that moment he wanted nothing more than to see her face.

—Well, come on then, she said, and lifted her hand.

For the first time he thought he heard an embarrassment in her voice. Suddenly she appeared small in the bay.

So he stepped into the water. He waded toward her and climbed into the canoe. He felt the cool and the damp of her hand as she guided him behind her.

His trousers were drenched. She smiled. She was holding a paddle made of tin and a broken broom handle. An empty bucket and a net lay beside her feet.

She tipped her hat back and paused, turning to him and looking down at her palms.

—Yohan, she said. I'm not very good at this.

She fell silent. The sounds of the village came to them and the girl with the soccer ball stood on the log and waited.

They left the bay, heading out into the ocean. It was not yet dusk, the daylight still bright on them and the water. He was sitting behind her and as they followed the coast toward the hill town, the long shadow of her hat swept her shoulders.

The heat of the day was replaced by a wind. He felt the push of the canoe. He watched the seawater drying on her back. The movement of her hands. The spread of the boat's wake. The sea was calm and he dipped his fingers into it.

Nearing the harbor, he saw the town as he had that first time. All the ships and all the homes. A thousand windows. And he looked up at the top of the hill, where there was now a star in the tree. It hovered there in the leaves, blinking, and then he lost it.

He thought she would enter the harbor. Instead she continued to follow the coast where a boy was closing umbrellas, one by one, their white and red stripes vanishing.

—Bia, he said, leaning forward. Where is Santi?

But she did not respond, she kept moving, and he thought of rivers. He thought of the ones he had rested beside and traveled across and the ones that had taken the lives of men. He thought of the speed and the shapes of water.

And he said, —Bia. Stay this time.

And she paddled once and stopped. He grew still and as they drifted away from the town he watched the shape of her there, rising. She lifted her arms for balance. Then she made her way toward him, across the length of the canoe, as lights appeared and the evening started.

Acknowledgments

> The train came out of the long tunnel
> into the snow country.
>
> —YASUNARI KAWABATA

Thank you to my family, Ethan Rutherford, Nayon Cho, Russell Perreault, Don Lee, Michael Collier, Ann Patchett, Joan Silber, Kate Walbert, Hannah Tinti, Sarah Shun-Lien Bynum, Lauren Groff, Caroline Casey, Jill Meyers, The National Book Foundation, The Bennington Writing Seminars, Sven Birkerts, Victoria Clausi, Dawn Dayton, Brian Morton, Amy Hempel, my dear Bret Anthony

Johnston, Simon & Schuster, Jonathan Karp, Richard Rhorer, Wendy Sheanin, Andrea DeWerd, Tracey Guest, Jessica Zimmerman, Rebecca Marsh, Jackie Seow, Christopher Lin, Irene Kheradi, Gina DiMascia, Joy O'Meara, Loretta Denner, Jane Elias, Emily Graff, WME, Laura Bonner, Shaun Dolan.

To Marysue (and Thea), for the leap.

And to Bill, always, for the embrace.

About the Author

Paul Yoon was born in New York City. His first book was the story collection *Once the Shore*. It was selected as a *New York Times* Notable Book and a Best Debut Fiction by National Public Radio, and it won the Asian American Literary Award and the 5 under 35 award from the National Book Foundation.